Come Home for Christmas, Cowboy

Come Home for Christmas, Cowboy

A Montana Born Christmas Novella

Megan Crane

TULE
PUBLISHING

Chapter One

O N DECEMBER 21st, the night of her thirtieth birthday, Christina Grey Cooper decided that it was finally time to stop lying to herself.

She was sitting in a very loud bar filled with people who made her feel deeply judgmental in a neighborhood she knew was filled with more of the same: trendy hipsters, as far as the eye could see, like the creeping vines that choked her mother's trellis in Marietta, Montana every summer. She was furthermore in Denver, Colorado, a city she never would have chosen for herself and yet had lived in for more than five years anyway.

And what did Christina have to show for the loyalty and love that had brought her here? To a bar bristling with ironic facial hair in a mile high city that still didn't feel like home? She cast a considering glance around at her surroundings, and tallied it all up in her head.

She didn't have the babies she'd always wanted and had expected to start having well before her thirties hit. She lived in a rented house she'd never liked much in a neighborhood that was convenient for Dare and his academic pursuits, but not so much for her and her daily commute to the other side of Denver—not that she'd ever bothered to complain, because how would that help anything? She had a journalism degree that she didn't use at her job as an office manager for a very small and boring commercial architectural firm, which she'd gotten purely to pay the bills Dare's doctoral program stipend and assorted grants couldn't cover. She wasn't chasing down important stories or writing much of anything at all, in fact, which was what she'd always thought she'd be doing with her life, with or without kids.

These days, she used her journalism degree purely to compose overtly jovial Facebook updates, the better to pretend her life was *awesome*. And online, it was. She made sure of it. Offline, she was addicted to all kinds of things. Angsty teen-oriented television shows. Erotically charged romance novels featuring often-paranormal men with control issues and ferocious, possibly life-threatening passions. Inappropriately fancy shoes from Zappos that she could wear around the house at night to feel like a queen with a glass of wine or three, then return for free come morning.

And, of course, she had Dare.

She eyed him then, sitting there across the table from her doing his best impression of a man all alone.

Dare, who she still loved with that roaring sort of fire inside of her that only hurt, these days. Dare, who she still wanted as much as she ever had, because she was a masochist, apparently. Dare, who didn't look like the microbiologist he was—whatever microbiologists were supposed to look like. He looked like a cowboy. Lanky and lean and darkly gorgeous, with that surprisingly lush mouth and distant dark blue gaze, like the far horizons were inside him, somehow. He looked like what and who he was, Darius James Cooper, the son of a coal miner from Gillette, Wyoming, who'd grown up hard and tough beneath wide open skies.

Dare, who also happened to have the quickest, sharpest, most impressive brain Christina had ever encountered.

She'd fallen in wild lust with Dare the moment she'd seen him sauntering across the University of Montana campus that early fall night in Missoula way back when, in his battered old jeans and an old grey t-shirt, that crooked smile of his that made his smoky blue eyes gleam poking out from beneath his dark brown hair.

She'd fallen in love with him shortly thereafter, sitting out beneath the dark canopy of a bright and breathless Montana night, while he talked to her in that deceptively lazy way of his about all the reasons he wanted to become a scientist.

And all that before he'd kissed her in that slow, patient, toe-curlingly *certain* way of his, which had made her so dizzy she'd almost fallen down. *Would have* fallen down, had Dare not caught her.

She'd believed—without question—that he always would.

Dare, who had married her in a ceremony that had made

them both shake with giddy laughter one weekend in Vegas because they couldn't afford to do anything but elope in the cheapest "chapel" around. Dare, who had spent all of their money on a ring Christina didn't need, but treasured nonetheless throughout all the months of Ramen and rice they'd eaten to pay it off.

Dare, the husband who hadn't acted as if he liked her in a very, very long time, now that she was allowing herself to consider it.

The truth was that she hadn't *wanted* to consider it.

This, Christina understood tonight—with a flash of un-wanted clarity as she stared across the suspiciously sticky table at her surly and silent husband while he nursed his beer and kept his dark, brooding attention on anything and everything but her—was the story of her life. This *was* her life. This was what it had been for longer than she liked to admit, and what it would be for as long as she held on.

And she'd been holding on—if only by her fingernails—for ages now.

Happy birthday to me, she thought then, her gaze on Dare while his was on whatever it was he saw when he didn't want to see her.

Christina had spent the whole day convincing herself that everything was *fine*. That *of course* Dare hadn't forgotten her birthday the way he'd forgotten everything else lately. And by *lately*, she really meant the past year and a half. She'd told herself that the fact he'd come home so late the night before and left before she'd climbed out of the shower this morning—making certain he saw as little of her as possible, she'd finally concluded after months of this kind of behavior—meant that he had some or other exciting thirtieth birthday surprise in the works.

That had taken some pretty desperate mental contortions on her part, but by this point, Christina was so good at contorting that she was practically a yoga master.

Because she knew he hadn't planned anything. If she'd really thought otherwise, she wouldn't have called him at his lab that afternoon. Not on his direct line or his cell phone, both of which she knew he'd send straight to voicemail the minute he saw her name, but through the front desk so the call would be transferred to him and he wouldn't be able to use his Caller ID to avoid her.

Happy and healthy people, she couldn't help but think, didn't worry about Caller ID or plan their phone calls like black ops attacks. They probably called their husbands whenever they felt like it. Without having to *contort*.

Moreover, their husbands probably just answered their goddamned phones—something, now that she was letting herself think about these things, Dare hadn't done in ages. She couldn't remember the last time they'd talked on the phone at all without her having to perform a whole choreographed series of her little yoga moves, in fact.

Happy and healthy, she thought now, *we certainly are not.*

"What are we doing tonight for my birthday?" Christina

MEGAN CRANE

had asked him cheerfully when he'd answered the phone.

She was always cheerful when she spoke to Dare these days. The quieter and darker and surlier he got, the more she turned herself into Pollyanna—the psychotically perky Energizer Bunny version that made her feel crazy and didn't even work on him, but what was the alternative? Meeting his darkness with more darkness? They'd black out the entire Denver Metropolitan Area.

"My thirtieth birthday!" she'd said as if he'd said something or required more information, so happily it had given her an immediate piercing headache. "Hooray!"

Yes, she'd actually said *hooray*. Out loud, as if she was the embodiment of a teen girl's text message. That was how desperate things had become.

Dare had sighed, heavily.

That was how he communicated now. Deep sighs and rolled eyes. Muttered things Christina couldn't quite hear but suspected she didn't much *want* to hear. If she squinted and pretended hard enough, though, *everything was fine*. Like those photos she took on her phone with the filter that blurred out everything but the one small part she wanted to focus on, then posted to Facebook with a long wake of exclamation points and emoticons. That was how she held on to her marriage. She filtered. She posted. She chose to believe her own carefully curated version of her life.

He didn't *say* anything. They didn't *fight*. They were *fine*.

Yay!!!!!!!! :) :) :) :) :)

But tonight she seemed to have lost her filter.

"Fine, Christina," he'd said after one of those long pauses of his, during which she could practically *see* the way he rubbed a hand over his face as if he was right there in front of her, exasperated by her. This, too, was their new normal. "I'll be home around eight."

So really, it was Christina's own fault that she was sitting in this terrible bar that she suspected Dare knew perfectly well she hated. He might even have chosen it for that very purpose, as revenge for her temerity in demanding he spend a single evening with her out of the past five hundred. It was her fault that she'd dressed up for the great occasion. Not the occasion of her birthday, for which Dare had naturally bought her nothing but a too-sweet pink drink, but the fact that the two of them were out somewhere together. *Almost* like the real couple they'd been approximately nine million years ago. It was her own fault that she'd put on mascara and the perfume he'd once growled in her ear drove him so crazy he could hardly control himself.

He'd been in complete control, of course, when he'd looked at her with that blank expression on his face when he'd walked in the back door at eight-thirty, making Christina feel deeply pathetic for once again allowing hope to triumph over experience.

Christina didn't feel pathetic at the moment. Not any longer. She felt annoyed—at herself.

She could have been curled up on the couch right now, enjoying a birthday evening with her Kindle and a glass of wine and possibly a selection of cupcakes from her favorite bakery. That would have been a great deal more fun than sitting in a crowded bar listening to a bad cover band ruin "Rockin' Around the Christmas Tree" while her husband—still the most beautiful creature she'd ever seen, even surly and distant and refusing to meet her eyes—looked like he was made of impenetrable granite.

Dare looked like that a lot, lately. Maybe all the time, in fact—it was just that Christina saw so little of him, "all the time" was only a few sporadic moments here and there, collected over weeks.

This is my life, she thought again, harder. *This... sad little mess.*

A terrible rendition of an overplayed holiday song and a sticky table, in a city she'd never liked that much, doing things she didn't care about at all, with a man who hadn't seemed to like *her* in a long time, and was—if she was really going to look at it the way she'd been avoiding doing for a long time now, with no filter and no overly curated Facebook bullshit—almost certainly cheating on her.

She let that settle on her, that nasty truth she'd been working so hard to avoid.

That was what all of these things meant when she looked at them as a whole, didn't they? Dare had always been a distracted scientist, a dreamy academic type with his head a million miles away, trying to cure the incurable. But this wasn't *distracted*. This was disinterested, disengaged. Passive aggressive and annoyed. This spelled *another woman.* It had to, didn't it?

Christina had known that for a long time, too, somewhere deep inside where it hurt too much to bear.

But tonight she was thirty, and it was almost Christmas, and she couldn't seem to do anything else but face it. Face everything, in fact. All her filters were off. All her protective walls had finally fallen down.

And she felt... nothing.

Mildly annoyed. A little bit tired. Cranky about the loud, bad band and the sticky table. But other than that? Nothing at all.

Which was how Christina knew, finally, that this had to stop. That she had to let go before there was nothing left of her. Before she really was nothing more than a perky Facebook update surrounded by smiley faces, and utterly empty within.

She was done contorting herself to please a man who couldn't be pleased—who didn't *want* to be pleased. Not by her, anyway. It didn't matter how much weight she lost or gained, how often she went to Pilates class or baked him coffee cake she'd then eat herself, or how scrupulously neat and clean she kept the ugly little rental house he avoided like the plague. It didn't matter how often she cooked his favorite meals, how cheerfully she spoke to him, or how carefully she made sure to avoid any kind of fight or disagreement or *intensity* of any kind.

As if it could get any worse. As if *this* wasn't bad enough.

Christina had made herself into a walking, talking pretzel for this man, and to what end? He lounged there, that dark and haunted look on his face, his eyes smoky and far-away, as if being with her was like being a jail sentence he had to endure. When she knew perfectly well that if anyone was trapped in this marriage, it was her.

Dare was about five seconds away from a PhD and the life he'd always wanted and had worked so hard to achieve. Christina was just… his wife. Which she'd been perfectly fine with until he'd forgotten her and the fact they were supposed to be a team.

She felt more than mildly annoyed then—she felt like throwing her overpriced and overly sweet drink right at his heartbreakingly gorgeous face. But that would take energy. Passion. That wildness inside of her that Dare had once made sing, and had now gone silent like everything else. She felt nothing.

She felt flat. *Flattened.*

"I hate yoga," she informed him. "I hate *contorting.*"

Dare shot a look across the table as if he hadn't expected her to speak, and might even be a little bit startled that she had, but he only shook his head.

Christina didn't know what he saw when he looked at her now. She saw the past. *Their* past. She saw the night he'd held her face between his hands and whispered, so fiercely, that he'd never loved anything in his life until her and didn't expect he'd ever love anything else, ever. She could feel the way he'd touched her, as if she'd been created specifically for him and he couldn't get enough of her. She remembered the slow, heated way he'd looked at her when they'd returned to their hotel room in Vegas, husband and wife at last. And what had come after.

God, the ways he'd touched her, once upon a time.

Whatever he saw tonight, it didn't show on his face. Then again, Christina thought as she looked—really looked—at that closed-off, granite expression of his, maybe it did.

Dare indicated her drink with his chin, his gaze flinty in all the commotion of the bar around them, and her heart felt raw.

"Are you about ready to get out of here?"

And she was. She really was.

HE WAS GONE by the time Christina woke up the next morning.

As usual.

There wasn't even a dent in the sofa cushions in the den, so maybe he hadn't even slept in the house. This, too, seemed like more evidence, all of it pointing to the same conclusion.

Christina waited for that to hurt, but it didn't. Which

was all the answer she needed, wasn't it?

So she packed up what little remained of herself into the tiny hatchback she'd bought with her own money that summer after college, she left a brief note telling him she wasn't coming back because she doubted he'd notice her absence otherwise, and she started driving north.

It took about ten hours, winter weather permitting, to drive to her hometown of Marietta, Montana, where her parents and sister and assorted other Grey family relatives lived. She drove out of Denver and into Wyoming on I-25, uninterrupted by any frantic phone calls from her husband. He probably didn't know she'd left him yet and was, she reminded herself harshly and repeatedly as she left her life with him behind her, highly unlikely to care if he did.

This was probably what he wanted. She should want it, too—and she thought she probably would, when she had a little more time to get used to the idea. When she was ready to accept that she'd finally given up on him.

When she was something other than numb.

Christina listened to the mixes she'd made while she and Dare were back in college together, all of which she'd loaded onto their computer a few years ago when she'd been trying to *feng shui* their life—another failed experiment in making Dare happy despite his clear preference to be anything but, which had been her primary occupation for most of their time in Denver.

Damn him.

She turned the music up loud and drove much too fast through the snow-covered grasslands of eastern Wyoming, not far from the place Dare came from and claimed he loathed deep unto his soul. She didn't want any of that in her head anymore—as if Dare's emotional history was stamped on the barren, winter-razed land itself. As if she had to look through him to see it.

Christina blocked out that unsettling notion and sang along to the songs that had once filled her with so much emotion they'd actually *hurt* to hear. She listened to Landry Bell sing a quiet song about a hard, painful love he couldn't give up even though he knew he should. She heard Trisha Yearwood sing about hearts wrapped up in armor, Keith Urban apologize to his love for his terrible behavior, and Tim and Faith sing about ignoring each other after a bad break up.

Christina tried to cry. She *wanted* to cry. She waited for that tidal wave of emotion to wash through her, to make her pull over to the side of the cold, lonely highway and sob and shake and wail. To feel as if she couldn't breathe, the way she had when Dare had broken up with her after he'd graduated and was interning at a lab an hour south of Missoula in Hamilton, Montana.

Back then, she'd fallen to pieces. She'd been twenty-one. She'd thought losing him would *kill her*. She'd curled up on her bed and sobbed until the tears wouldn't come anymore, and then she'd stayed there in the fetal position. She hadn't felt right for the whole two days it had taken for them to get back together. And she'd known then that she'd never be whole unless she was with him. Never.

I love you, he'd said. *I'll never leave you again.*

See that you don't, she'd murmured against his neck.

And he'd kept that promise, hadn't he? *Jerk.*

But Christina didn't cry today, no matter what songs she played, and she felt whole and fairly hearty, too, all things considered. No matter how she tried to feel tragic. No matter how glum the weather was when she reached Billings, Montana, where her horn dog Uncle Billy lived with the woman he'd unapologetically stolen from his own son, Christina's cousin Jesse, and then married and impregnated. And maybe not in that order.

"I have my own map of emotional pain," she reminded herself out loud as she headed west on I-90 toward Livingston, following the great Yellowstone River as it wound its way toward Marietta and beyond to Bozeman. Slowly, surely, the Great Plains became the Rocky Mountains. *Her* Rocky Mountains—the Absaroka-Beartooths and the Crazies as the plains gave way—not the Colorado Rockies down in Denver that weren't quite the same and weren't quite right no matter how many years she'd lived there. And she'd been on the road for hours, so she kept right on talking to herself. "Everywhere I look in Montana, there's another part of me. Not *Dare and me.* Just me."

Her family had been in Montana for generations. Greys

had come across these same plains in covered wagons in the 1800s, leaving far worse things behind in Boston than one surly husband who was probably—almost definitely—cheating on her with one of his fellow doctoral candidates. At least Christina had a heater in her old car and the ability to stop in gas stations to stock up on sugary, salty, highly-processed road food for her journey.

And the sad truth was, she felt fine, more or less. Better than she had in years, because this was the first day in a long, long time she hadn't lied to herself about a single thing. She might not feel entirely herself, but then she'd had a long time to get used to that, hadn't she? Maybe that was what growing up was. Maybe that's all this was, too: her childish infatuation with Dare finally running its inevitable course.

Maybe this had been coming from the start. Maybe they should have stayed broken up all those years ago. Maybe she was only just catching up.

She jammed her foot down on the gas pedal. Because it was December 23rd and dark outside already, and after all this time wasted, all these years lost, Christina just wanted to get home.

DARE SAT IN his truck outside the dark house, and knew.

She'd finally done it. She'd finally left him.

He didn't have to go inside the shitty little house she'd worked so hard to make a home. He didn't have to look for empty spaces where the signs of her had been. He already knew. He already felt it creeping through his body like frost, chilling him to the bone.

The house was dark. Cold. In all the years he'd known Christina, he'd never come home to a dark house. She'd always, always left the light burning for him, even on those nights he'd muttered not to expect him or had simply stayed away until dawn.

He supposed he'd started to imagine she always would. That she'd just… take it, all the crap he'd dumped on her, forever and ever.

Had he really thought that?

Dare's hands tightened around the wheel, and he couldn't seem to move. He couldn't climb out of the truck and go into the house, because that would make it real. Inside that house was the life he'd decided he needed to live, the one without her that he'd never cared for much when he'd experienced it before, and the worst part was, she had no idea that he was doing her a favor. That he was saving her.

She thought what he'd wanted her to think. That he was done with her. That he was no longer in love with her.

If she'd left him, she must finally hate him.

Or, even worse, he'd succeeded in taking all of that joy and heat and love away from her at last, the way he'd shoved it outside himself in order to do this, and left her with nothing inside for him—for them—but all of that darkness.

His darkness.

He was such an asshole, it made him ache. It made his whole body hurt, like the flashing onset of one of the viruses he studied. He wished he didn't know better. He wished it would just kill him, so he could escape his own head, the cold, dark finality of his own actions. His own terrible fate.

He couldn't bring himself to go inside. He didn't want to confirm his success, at last. He couldn't accept that after all of this, after all this time, she'd finally gone and done what he'd pushed her to do.

What he'd been so damned sure he wanted her to do.

Until now.

So instead, Dare backed the truck out of the driveway, pulled out into the street, tried to keep breathing though he could hardly see the point without Christina, and went after her.

Chapter Two

"**Y**OU LEFT."

Christina didn't have to turn around to identify that low, accusatory voice, burned as it was into her very bones, and so she didn't. She stood very still, scowling into the interior of her parents' refrigerator as if that might make a tube of cookie dough appear before her where there was only a half-eaten tuna casserole in Tupperware, and waited.

Because maybe she was still sound asleep upstairs in her childhood bedroom and this was but a dream. Maybe Dare wasn't really standing there in her parents' kitchen doorway in a cloud of December cold at six-thirty-three on the Tuesday morning the day after she'd left him, when she hadn't expected he would notice she'd left for at least a week. Maybe two weeks. Or maybe not at all, if he decided to "stay at the lab" indefinitely.

She certainly hadn't imagined he'd care enough about her absence to drive ten hours north to Marietta. This had to be a dream.

But he shouldered his way inside and closed the door behind him with an emphatic click that echoed in her head like a gunshot then scraped over her as if she'd narrowly missed the bullet. And she had to accept that yes, he was really there. *Right there.* He'd chased after her, apparently. She couldn't believe it. She didn't.

And to spite her, her heart lurched a little bit at the sight of him. That was why it took her a minute to process that tone of his. As if *he* was angry. At *her.*

Surely not.

"All your stuff seems to be packed in that car out in your parents' driveway," Dare continued when she didn't say anything or look at him directly. And he seemed so *big,* then—looming there out of the corner of her eye, lanky and dark and that smoky gaze of his fixed on her—that the familiar old kitchen seemed to shrink tight around him. Around her, too, much as she tried to pretend otherwise. "I could see it through the windows. Did you move out, Christina? Without bothering to tell me first?"

Old habits died hard, because her first, immediate reaction was panic.

She was *panicked,* not that he was apparently in the mood to be both talkative and confrontational, but that she was letting him see her like this. Her dark hair was in a scruffy bun on the top of her head. She was completely unshowered after a long, restless night. And she was wearing not just her ratty old yoga pants and a long-sleeved PBR championship t-shirt she'd bought at a bull riding event back in high school and had found stuffed in a drawer in the old bedroom she'd shared throughout her childhood with her older sister, Luce—but a pair of horrible, bright blue wool socks her mother had knitted during her "amateur knitwear as gifts" phase.

Her pulse raced with sheer, dizzying anxiety at the idea that presenting him with anything less than herself as perfect as humanly possible would *prove it*—prove that he was right to have stopped loving her. Her heart pounded so hard and so high she thought it might choke her.

Christina had to remind herself—sharply—that she'd left him at last. It was over. It didn't matter what she looked like. Or how beautiful he was, even when he was glaring at her like that, drilling holes in the side of her head. Or that this was the first time in ages that he'd actually looked at her, by choice, for more than two derisive seconds in a row.

"I'm sorry," she said, when the silence had dragged on a good, long stretch, and Dare was still there and still watching her in that way of his, dark and much too intense at once, which she could feel perfectly well even while she was pretending to be *consumed* by the contents of the fridge. "You haven't voluntarily spoken to me in so long. I'd forgotten what that sounded like."

"Here I am, Christina. You want to talk to me? Go for it."

Everything inside of her clenched tight and then *hurt*. Christina told herself it was anger, nothing more. Righteous indignation, in fact. But she didn't want to give him the satisfaction of seeing her upset. She didn't want to *contort.* Ever again.

She let the refrigerator door fall shut and pivoted, scowling at the full sight of him to cover the way her heart leaped even higher and pounded harder. Because peripheral vision couldn't possibly do him justice. Dare glared back at her, so tall and so beautiful, even with a rough night's beard on his jaw and that intense, shattering look in his gorgeous eyes. Even his jeans looked tired, and his dark hair was spiky, as if he'd been running his fingers through it all the way north, the way he did when he was agitated, though his big, hard hands were thrust in his pockets now.

All of this told her things she didn't want to know, and didn't believe anyway.

Not anymore. Christina was done believing. She was done with faith. She was certainly done with parsing the many dark moods of one Darius James Cooper as if that was her primary job.

She was *done.*

"That sounded almost belligerent, Dare," she said, pleased she sounded so cool. So unbothered. "But I know that can't be true. Because what on earth do *you* have to be mad about?"

"You really want to ask me that after I drove ten hours in the middle of the night to get here?"

"No one asked you to do that. I stopped asking you for anything a long time ago, you might have noticed." She shrugged, a brittle jerk of one shoulder. "Or not."

She didn't recognize that glitter in his smoky eyes then, much less the leaping thing inside her that made her stomach clench tight.

"So let me make sure I understand what's happening here," he said softly, with an undercurrent of something darker in his low voice. "The last time I saw you, in Denver, where we live and which is over six hundred and fifty miles south of where we're standing right now, you were having a major attitude because you wanted a big birthday party."

"I did not want a big birthday party. I didn't want a party at all—I wanted my husband to acknowledge my birthday." *And by extension, me*, she thought, but did not say. She lifted her chin and tried to keep her teeth from grinding together. "They're not the same thing."

"You didn't like the place we went. Not that you said so or offered any suggestions about where else to go, mind you—I was supposed to pick that up by telepathy. You sat there like a pissed off princess, mad and quiet, like you've been doing for months now."

"I thought your doctorate was in microbiology, Dare, not creative writing," she seethed at him, losing her grip on remaining anything like cool. "And nice try, but you're not going to *argue* me into your version of the last couple of years. I was there. I remember what actually happened."

"And then I come home from a long day at the lab and you're gone. Just… gone. Boom. Without warning. Certainly without any conversation."

She crossed her arms over her chest. "I left a note."

"A note." His voice was incredulous and deeply pissed at once, and there was no reason at all that it should skid through her like that, like hunger. Like a kind of need she'd thought had died a long time ago. Christina had to pull in a breath before she shuddered. "We've been together for over a decade, married for more than half that time, and when you decided you were done you... left me a note."

"If you needed me to explain the contents of the note to you, you could have called," she pointed out. "Rather than leaping in your truck and chasing me here to make up some fantasy version of our life where I'm the spoiled drama queen and you're the bewildered, innocent party."

His gaze felt like a touch from all the way across the kitchen, and she hated how much she wanted to relent. To go to him, hold him—anything to stop this. But she couldn't do that. She couldn't let herself give in. Because she'd only end up right back here again. She knew it.

"And what would have happened if I'd called you?" Dare asked, into the rising tension in the room, sharper than the cold outside.

"You mean, other than me swerving into oncoming traffic on the interstate because I haven't heard your ring tone in so long?"

His smoky eyes narrowed, and that mouth of his was firm. "Would you have done that aggressively perky thing you've been doing lately? Like a morning talk show host?"

That smarted, she could admit it, because it was a direct hit. But it didn't change the facts.

"What do you want, Dare?" she asked, her voice clipped even to her own ears. "Why are you here?"

"You took your belongings and disappeared while I was at work," he said gruffly, and she had the impression he'd been repeating that to himself over and over again throughout his long drive. It had the sound of a catch phrase, more than a comment. "That's the way people leave abusive relationships, Christina. It's the way people *escape*. How exactly does that apply here?"

She didn't know what to do, suddenly. The impulse that had pushed her into her car and into that long, bleak, cold drive had deserted her somewhere around Casper, Wyoming. She felt hollow. Which wasn't at all the same thing as numb, it turned out. For one thing, hollow *hurt*. And it had never occurred to her that he would come after her. Or that he'd be pissed off at her if he did.

There was a part of her that desperately wanted that to *mean something*.

"What did you expect me to do?" Christina was furious that her voice came out like that then, nothing but a harsh little scrape into the early morning.

"I don't know." His voice was dark, but the look in his eyes was worse. Much worse. She felt something turn over inside of her, and was afraid it was too much like shame. "I might have tried *having a conversation* before I fled across state lines."

"Who is she?" she asked, because really, that was the crux of it, wasn't it? All the rest of this was sound and fury. And so what if she didn't really want to know the answer? She wanted to stand here and have him rail at her as if *she* was the problem in their marriage even less.

"What?"

"The woman. Whoever you're cheating with." Christina found that when she said it out loud, when she made it real, whatever emotional distance she'd thought she'd been maintaining exploded into something much more gristly and tight and close within her, making her chest constrict and her vision blur. "Whoever keeps you warm all those nights you sleep somewhere else. I'm assuming it's someone from the lab. Some smart PhD scientist type just like you, far more appropriate to your new station in life, presumably. You never struck me as into bimbos." She let out a sound far too painful to be a laugh. "Then again, I never thought you'd cheat on me, I'll admit."

For a moment, he looked as if she'd clubbed him over the head. Then he blinked, and he looked nothing so much as grim. And if possible, even more furious than before.

"I'm not cheating on you, Christina."

It was the way he said it that made her stop and blink that rush of emotion away so she could see him clearly again. That stark, harsh, appalled tone. That look on his face, as if she'd plunged a jagged knife deep into his chest and it hurt but he was too angry to notice.

She believed him.

And for one second, that felt like light, pouring in like summer from above. Relief, sweet and pure.

But then she thought about it and realized that if there was no other woman, if Dare had been behaving like this simply because he felt like behaving like this, that made it all significantly worse.

"I see," she said. She did not see. "So you just… hate me? Is that it?"

Dare let out one of those exasperated sighs of his, and he might as well have punched her. She thought she could live another three lives in rapid succession without hearing that sound again. It made her shrivel inside.

It made her want to punch him, and for real this time.

"I don't hate you," he said, sounding impatient, though his gaze looked a whole lot more like tortured. "I don't—" He shook his head, and then raked his hands through the fall of his thick, messy dark hair, and Christina would have given a great deal to know what he'd *almost* said just then. "You didn't have to run back home to your parents at a moment's notice because you didn't like how one night went."

"You can't possibly think that if you keep acting like this was all me, I'll start believing you, can you? Because it doesn't work that way." She pointed at him because it was the next best thing to walloping him. Better, because she didn't think touching him was a good idea. Touching him had never led to anything but trouble. More than ten years of trouble. "I'm not the one who's spent more time at the lab than at home. The one who stopped speaking. The one who hasn't touched his wife in months. The one who rolls his eyes every time I speak. I wasn't running back home to my parents, Dare. I was running away from you."

And Christina finally understood, in that moment, what that hollowness inside her meant. Because it was one thing to have a broken heart. At least the heart was still in there, if shattered, doing its job in pieces.

Dare had ripped hers out and stamped it into oblivion, and she didn't see how there was any coming back from that.

And the look he was giving her then made her want to cry.

He swallowed, hard.

"I wasn't cheating on you," he said then, his voice gruffer than she'd ever heard it. "I don't break my promises, especially to you. You know that."

She got it, then. In a big, nauseating sort of slide into clarity. It made the polished wood floor seem to rock beneath her feet.

"Is that what this was?" she threw at him, somewhere between *aghast* and simply *hurt*. "Were you deliberately pushing me away so I'd be the one to break the promises here?" She was so upset then she thought it must have been rolling off of her, like the heat from the radiator that hugged the floorboards around the edges of the room. "What's the matter, Dare? You got what you wanted. You should be thrilled."

"This is me," he growled at her. "Fucking ecstatic."

And the tension in the room seemed to ripple, then grow, demanding that one of them break it by any means necessary, just to relieve the terrible weight of it—

The back door flew open again with a great *woosh*, slamming against the far wall and making Christina jump. Actually jump into the air, then plaster herself back against the refrigerator when she hit ground.

And for a moment it was nothing but cold air and commotion. Her sister Luce charged inside like she was a heat-seeking missile. She shepherded her three boys in front of her while her two big dogs bounded all around the four of them, and was dispensing orders left and right like a drill sergeant as she went.

Christina's nephews were a blur of pure boy energy ranging in age from an irrepressible ten down to a Tasmanian Devil-like six, and they all shouted greetings to Dare and Christina and complaints to their mother at the same high volume as they careened inside, each dragging backpacks and what looked like camping supplies in their wake. The dogs, both of unknown mutt origin with sloppy grins and too much triumphant barking, ran circles in and around the wake of the rowdy trio like a kind of rough and tumble holiday parade.

And it was only a reprieve, Christina was well aware as she dispensed hugs to three sticky little bodies in motion. A small intermission, and she was perfectly happy not to look at Dare as it happened. Because she had no idea how to resist him. She'd finally come to terms with the quiet, distant husband she'd thought was cheating on her. She'd come to terms with it last night and she'd made the decision to leave him.

This Dare, she barely recognized, but he reminded her way too much of the man she'd fallen in love with all those years ago. And she knew exactly how dangerous that was. There was contorting—and then there was melting. And Dare had always been really, really talented at making her melt down into a puddle whether she wanted to or not.

"Into the den!" Luce was ordering as she kicked the door shut behind her, slinging a couple of overstuffed duffel bags on the floor of the kitchen, near their mother's prized wooden table where all the best meals of their childhood had been conducted. "You have five minutes, guys. *Five minutes* and then we head out!"

And then she pulled her hat off of her head, let her shining blonde hair—long the bane of Christina's existence, it was so effortlessly pretty no matter how little attention Luce paid to it, unlike Christina's own red-streaked dark hair that was best left to its own devices—tumble down around her shoulders like sunshine on a bitterly cold winter morning like this one, and blinked back and forth between Dare and

Christina in the sudden silence.

"What are you guys doing here?" Luce asked finally, when it became painfully clear that no one else was going to speak. "I thought you said you couldn't do Christmas back home with the family this year."

"Nice to see you, too," Christina murmured, trying to pull herself together—or out of that heart-pounding tension, anyway. She didn't look at Dare, who'd always found family in general and Luce in particular a bit of a challenge at times. After all, he hadn't spoken to his own relatives since he'd left home at eighteen.

And Luce was Christina's best friend in the entire world, always had been and ever would be, but *challenging* was the least of what she was when she got going. It was a Grey family trait, Christina knew: hardheadedness to their own detriment and an utter lack of respect for the tough lessons of their own family history.

Luce frowned at them both. "You look like you're in the middle of divorce proceedings in Mom and Dad's kitchen, two days before Christmas."

"We're not getting divorced." Dare's voice was low and hard, and Christina felt the kick of it deep in her belly. And something much warmer that she didn't want to examine everywhere else.

But she still didn't look at him. "We're talking about it, in fact. Not that it's something we need to discuss as a group, if you don't mind, Luce. And where are Mom and Dad, anyway? Out on a trip?"

She hadn't thought it was particularly weird that her parents hadn't been here when she'd staggered in the night before, punchy from the long drive. Ryan and Gracie Grey had never locked their doors in all their lives here in Marietta just a ten minute walk from Main Street and they never would, so Christina had strolled in and made herself at home as if she was still sixteen and college and Dare had never happened.

And, if she was honest, she'd been relieved that she hadn't had to explain what was going on to anyone just yet. It made it all that little bit less real. She'd assumed her parents were off on one of the outdoor adventure trips they conducted all year long as part of the Montana Wilds Adventure Company they owned and ran from a shop above the bookstore in downtown Marietta.

"Season's pretty much done," Luce said, pulling off her gloves and shoving them deep in her coat pockets. She'd know, given she ran the shop. "There's some New Year's dog sledding thing, but we're not sure yet if Dad or Marshall McKenzie will run it. Mom and Dad went out to Big Sky to help Gram and Grandpa get the Big House ready for Christmas." She eyed the two of them, her slender body visibly tense beneath her winter coat. "And I'd hug you both, but you can't get a divorce. Not right now. That's completely unacceptable, I'm sorry."

"Your support is terrifying, Luce," Dare murmured, from

where he leaned against the kitchen counter, looking for all the world like a lazy cowboy, if Christina ignored that hard glint in his smoky gaze. "But appreciated."

Christina didn't bother glaring at him. She focused on her sister instead. "Are you really—What are you talking about?"

"It's Christmas," Luce said, as if that was all the explanation required. She held up a finger, then yelled toward the den. "Two minute warning, gentlemen! Start the countdown!" Then she faced Christina again. "You know how Mom gets if the magic of Christmas is threatened. You know it's a whole thing."

"I'm wearing the wool socks of doom right now." Christina stuck a foot out as evidence. "I'm *filled* with the Christmas spirit."

Luce shrugged, when normally she would have laughed. "So you see my point."

Christina couldn't keep herself from sneaking a look at Dare then, as if they were still a team. As if they ever had been. But his expression was carefully blank. Too carefully blank. Granite all the way through, again, and *that* felt like another, much harder kick, because he wasn't behaving the way she'd expected he would. The way she'd been so sure he would—and that was why she'd left him. She didn't have the slightest idea what to do about it.

But she couldn't punch him in front of her sister, as much as she might feel like it just then. Christina was the good daughter, the well-behaved sister, the child who had always done precisely what was expected of her, and happily. Luce was the belligerent loudmouth troublemaker of their little corner of the Grey family, a role she got away with because she was also willowy, slender, and shockingly beautiful. And well she knew it.

"Luce." Christina tried to exude a calm sort of authority she didn't feel. "Mom is a grown woman. I know she likes to get into the Christmas spirit with a vengeance, but she can handle a little bit of reality, even in December. I promise you."

Dare shifted audibly, but she refused to look at him. She refused.

"I kicked Hal's broke, cheating ass out," Luce announced with a kind of grim finality that made Christina feel the slightest little trickle of reluctant sympathy for the brother-in-law she hadn't been fond of since way back when they'd all been at Marietta High, when he'd been an overly-entitled member of the varsity football team and merely one of Luce's many boyfriends. But only a very little trickle, quickly gone. "Being the complete loser that he is, he'll probably spend Christmas drunk and cleaning out our house to see what he can sell to pay for more strippers. He likes strippers. And I'm pretty sure 'strippers' is a euphemism." She pulled in a breath that sounded far more ragged and painful than her harshly amused tone would suggest, but that was Luce. Hard like a rock on the outside despite how beautiful she was, and secretly breakable within. Far within. "I told him that if he's still there when we get back from Grandma and Grandpa's, I'll shoot him and save myself the trouble of arguing over the money he owes me in court. I'm kind of hoping he thinks I'm kidding."

She turned to yell at her sons again, and Christina couldn't help it. She looked over at Dare. He didn't *quite* widen those smoky eyes of his in return, and that felt too good. Much too good. As if they were communicating again—but a single glance didn't make up for all that silence. It couldn't. She recollected herself and jerked her treacherous gaze away. Then she tried to transmit the compassion she didn't entirely feel, not when she'd never wanted Hal for her sister in the first place, when Luce turned back again.

"So you understand," Luce said, as if they'd settled a critical point between them.

"I'm really sorry to hear that you and Hal broke up, if that's what you mean."

"No, you're not. You don't have to be so polite about it, Christina." Luce smoothed her hair back from her forehead and sighed. "You hated Hal ever since he snapped your bra in the ninth grade, and who can blame you?"

Christina tried to be diplomatic. "I always thought Hal had some impulse control issues, yes."

"That's what you call it when they're little shits in high school," Luce said then, and though she frowned Christina understood it wasn't directed at her. "Little shits who have three kids and no job? You begin to call it other things."

"Luce, I'm so sorry—"

"I'm not. I only married him because he knocked me up and my kids are worth putting up with anything, even their father." Luce stood straighter and her brown eyes burned, but she didn't crack. "Don't be sorry. Just don't be *this*." She waved her hand in the wide, cold, brutal space between Christina at the fridge and Dare by the counter. "I think one Grey family marriage on the rocks at a time is about all Mom is prepared to deal with, especially at this time of year. To say nothing of what Grandma will do if she find out *both* of us are about to be divorced."

Christina winced, which had no doubt been Luce's intention. Elly Grey was the fearsome matriarch of the Grey family and about as far from the stereotypical apple-cheeked, affectionate grandmother as it was possible to get. A whole lot more Calamity Jane than Mrs. Butterworth, Christina and her cousins had always joked—but never where Grandma might overhear.

And Grandma's two favorite topics of conversation, especially at holidays when she could gather the entire family together as her captive audience? One: the epic disappointment that was their Grandpa, renowned across the state of Montana and probably Idaho and Wyoming besides for his wandering eye. And two: the ways in which *most* of her four children, two of her three sons and her only daughter, had let her down with their terrible life choices. Luce and Christina's father Ryan was the only one of her children whose marriage *hadn't* fallen apart, and the only one Grandma ever spared her sharp tongue.

The favorite son, her uncles would mutter darkly at her father during the inevitable lecture on morals lost and promises kept at every single family gathering ever. *How sweet.*

Christina's mother Gracie would be heartbroken that both of her daughters' marriages had failed. Distraught all the way through, as if her own relationship was on the line. Grandma, on the other hand, would see it as nothing more than the validation she'd been waiting for that this next generation of Greys was as wretched as the one before it.

You're all cursed, she'd announced in her direst tones at last year's Thanksgiving meal. *You can thank your grandfather for that. Blood will tell.*

Thanks, Pop, her Uncle Jason had muttered in that dark, gruffly irritated way of his that kept the patrons of his bar, Grey's Saloon, under his control or swiftly back out on the streets of Marietta before they knew what hit them. *Have some potatoes. And the blame.*

Happy freaking holidays, indeed, Christina thought now. Grandma's bitterness was one of the reasons they hadn't driven up for Thanksgiving this year. That and the fact Dare had worked the entire holiday weekend and had suffered exactly fifteen minutes of Christina's makeshift attempt at a holiday meal before stalking off.

She'd eaten all the stuffing and gravy, gained five pounds in a day, and didn't regret a damned thing.

"Well," Christina said now, as briskly as she could. "Dare and I can't *pretend* to be happily married, Luce. Not even to avoid Grandma's wrath."

"Why not?" Luce pounced on that, her brown eyes gleaming in a way that Christina recognized from a thousand Luce-led 'adventures' in the past. She braced herself and sure enough, her sister kept talking. "Just until January. Who will it hurt? All you have to do is make it through the next few days. A week at most."

"What? No. Absolutely—"

"Sure." Dare sounded darkly amused and something else Christina didn't particularly want to identify. Certainly not right there in front of her sister, when so many things were happening inside of her she couldn't count them all. "We can do that."

She turned to look at him. Slowly, as if he'd transformed into an obstreperous elk while she'd been glaring at her sister. "Are you insane?"

Dare shrugged, his smoky gaze a challenge and his mouth in its little crook, and she still felt the wild *heat* of it. It still moved through her like a lick of pure flame.

It still felt like perfection.

The only difference was, she hated that it did. Her marriage had been nothing but a kamikaze death spiral for the last few years, it was destroying her, and she finally wanted it to stop.

Didn't she?

"Consider it a Christmas present to your whole family, Luce," Dare said, turning up the wattage on his smile and aiming it straight at Christina's poor, heartbroken sister, the jerk, when he hadn't smiled at *Christina* in ages. "It's the least Christina and I can do."

Chapter Three

D ARE HATED HOLIDAYS.

In his family, not getting his ass kicked or ending up in the ER after a family gathering was considered a major gift—if not a blessing—and that was rare enough. Pointed "family time" holidays had always been opportunities for high expectations that quickly fell apart and turned into entirely too much drunken brawling.

He'd opted out of that mess when he'd left. He'd opted out of all of it. The great, gnarled family tree made of alcoholics and violent lunatics, as far back as anyone had ever bothered to trace it. Not that his relatives spent a lot of time worried about their genealogy. It was pretty obvious. Go to Gillette, Wyoming, look around for the biggest wastes of human space involved in some or other depressingly public downward spiral, and that was likely to be a Cooper family gathering en route to another disaster.

He was sure it was why he'd started studying viruses as an undergraduate and become obsessed. Because he had the usual scientific fantasies of making the world a better place, sure. But also because his family was its own virus, for all intents and purposes, and he wanted the cure. His father had been made entirely of rage and paranoia and had been well-lubricated at all times by vast quantities of his beloved sour mash. Leroy Cooper had beaten the crap out of anything within his reach, with the family trademark of dark, sadistic glee. His own brothers. Random neighbors in their run-down trailer park. Anyone who looked at him funny, according to him. Dare's mother, who had never *not* looked at him funny, by Leroy's account. Dare himself, by virtue of existing.

Until Dare got big enough to challenge him back, that was—which was when Leroy had decided to enact his final cruelty. He'd taken himself out and had dragged Dare's brutalized mother with him one bullet after the next on a snowy March afternoon, right there in the living room of their trailer.

Fifteen year old Dare had been the one to find them, the one to call the police and report the tragedy. And as he'd stood there waiting for the cops to come and clean up yet another Cooper family mess, he'd stared down at what was left of the two people who should have loved him the most and he'd understood, deep down, that they hadn't been able to love anything. Not him. Not themselves. Just like everyone else in his world.

Just like him.

Because he was as infected as the rest of them. Dare knew that. Hell, he'd always known that, no matter the external differences between him and his down-and-out kin. They might still have been playing their desperate games back in Gillette while he'd lost himself in academics, but inside they were all the same. That awful truth had been stamped into his bones on a cold March afternoon more than fifteen years ago now, when his grandmother's response to his parents' murder/suicide had been to smack Dare in the face and complain about having to care for "another goddamned parasite." And he'd been as messed up as the rest of them, because he'd only laughed.

He'd only pretended he could ever be something other than a piece of shit no matter how many degrees he collected because Christina had always felt like an antidote to that poison in him. Like the cure he'd been looking for, if he was honest.

She still did. And it still rocked him all the way to that dark, dark hole where his soul should have been. But viruses didn't have cures, only antiviral remedies that never lasted long before the virus overcame them. Prevention was far better than any potential cure—and that meant Dare had been kidding himself. And he was standing here in her parents' house in Montana, so that meant he still was.

The day before Christmas Eve, no less.

Suffice it to say, he'd never really understood Christina and her family's fascination with Christmas, as if it was an annual miracle that could save souls when really, it was just a day. An overhyped day at that. Dare knew lost souls didn't happen back one day, no matter how many pine trees died for the cause.

This year was no different. Ryan and Gracie's house was already stuffed with enough holiday cheer to fell a battalion of elves. There were stockings over the fireplace. There had been reindeer with blinking lights out on the front lawn. There were evergreen garlands wrapped around the staircase railing leading up to the second floor and a fully decorated, gleaming tree in the living room, despite the fact no one would be here on the actual day of Christmas. Every Grey around packed up and headed out to Big Sky every year to spend Christmas Eve and Christmas Day with their intimidating grandparents and the rest of the extended family.

Dare would have said the Greys didn't exactly get along, but they didn't get into fistfights, either, so he supposed that was better than the so-called Christmases he'd suffered through as a kid. But he still didn't get it.

Now, standing here in his in laws' living room looking at all the handmade Christmas tree ornaments stitching together a patchwork of obviously happy family memories that made him feel itchy and restless by virtue of his proximity to them, it was even more baffling than usual.

Because he didn't want this. He knew better than this. Why was he here?

Why couldn't he let Christina go?

He never should have caved, years ago. He'd broken up with her when he'd graduated from college and he should have left things that way, because it had taken exactly one look at Christina Grey in Missoula to understand that she was forever. That she was every single one of the things he couldn't have, because he knew he'd destroy them. Home. Happiness. Family.

Love. Hope.

He'd known it that very first night. He'd known it when he'd kissed her. He'd certainly known it when that insane chemistry had erupted between them, blotting out everything but what they could do to each other in bed. He'd known it when he'd walked away from her and he'd known it when he'd given in to that howling thing inside of him and gotten back together with her, too.

He never should have stayed with her and he never should have married her, because he'd known from the start that this was where it would lead. She would want all the things he couldn't give her, he wouldn't have it in him to give them, and then what?

This, he told himself darkly. *This is what.*

He was a coward, just like his father before him. Christina was the warmest, brightest person he'd ever met. Her smile shifted the stars around in the sky above him without her even trying. He'd never laid a finger on her and he never would, but that didn't mean there weren't other ways of hurting people. He was a coward and a bastard besides, making her as lost and sad as he was. And here he was after she'd finally left him, lining up to do more damage. What the hell was wrong with him?

But he knew the answer to that. He always had.

He reached over and touched a big ornament made of orange construction paper and purple pipe cleaners that said her name in giant, loopy childish letters, as if it was some kind of magical talisman. She was his own personal bit of sunshine, his own magical spell, and she deserved to get every single thing she wanted.

And Dare couldn't give her any of them.

Not one.

But he still couldn't seem to leave her, either.

"I hope you're proud of yourself," Christina said from behind him, and she sounded neither warm nor bright then. He let go of the ornament and straightened, feeling as guilty as if she'd caught him at something truly illicit. "You've made a sad, painful situation into something far worse."

Luce had charged off into the cold morning with her pack of unruly creatures in tow, and Christina had stormed upstairs without another word to him. Dare had heard the shower go on and had let out a breath he hadn't known he'd been holding, because at least she hadn't kicked him back out the door when he'd walked in. He hadn't known how much he'd expected her to do exactly that until she hadn't.

"I'm looking at it as an opportunity," he said now, facing her.

He immediately wished he wasn't. She'd been cute enough in her pajamas, with her hair twisted back out of her way. But now she was dressed, and not in that strange, preppy-meets-plastic way she'd been dressing the last little while, all blow-dried hair and too much eye make up. Today she looked like his mountain girl again, in jeans, boots and a long-sleeved henley, her hair brushed but still wet at her shoulders, her face scrubbed clean of everything except her pretty eyes and that frown.

God, he loved this woman. He didn't know how to stop, no matter how destructive it was. No matter how little he knew what that word meant.

"An opportunity to do what?" she demanded. She stood at the bottom of the stairs, more in the foyer than in the living room, as if she didn't trust herself any closer to him. Or as if she didn't trust *him,* and he'd earned that, too. "Ruin every last thing I love?"

"Yes. That is my only goal."

There was a time she might have smiled at that, even in the middle of a fight. Not today.

"Congratulations," she said, her voice much too cold. "You've achieved it and then some."

"I accept that I deserve the gloves off."

"You said it, Dare," she snapped at him. "Not me."

"You want to hit me?" he asked softly. It was easier to be pissed than contrite—and he'd fed that part of himself all the way up from Denver. He let it move through him now, too. "Go right ahead. But you should know. If you put your hands on me, I won't necessarily keep mine off of you."

She blinked at him. "Oh, I'm sorry. Was that sexual? I can't remember what that's supposed to sound like. It's been nine hundred years."

He didn't mean to move toward her. But the truth was, he'd only been able to freeze her out when she'd let him. *This* version of his wife—spirited and bright even in the flare of her temper, the way he remembered her—he couldn't keep away from.

Then again, he didn't try that hard.

Christina stood her ground, but flushed when he came close and then even closer. He kept moving so she had to tip her chin up to keep looking him in the eye. And it had been so long. He felt as drunk as any one of his no-account uncles, wild with it and the spiraling sensation deep within him, telling him that if he didn't taste her right here, right now, he might never get the opportunity again.

"What are you doing?" she asked, and there was something solemn, nearly sacred, in the husky scrape of her voice in all the quiet. It lit him on fire.

He reached over and slid his hands over the perfect curves of her cheeks, feeling the way she fit so beautifully in his grip. She was little and delicate and made for him, and she still made him feel like he was the man he'd always wanted to become. It was why he'd stopped touching her. She made him *believe*.

And then, though it wasn't fair, he couldn't keep himself from asking the worst question. The one he didn't want to know the answer to. "Why did you let me do it?"

Christina sucked in a breath and he could feel the shock move through her, could see it in her dark eyes.

"*Let* you?" she hissed at him. "Are you crazy? *Let* you? I practically begged you to treat me like I was slightly more interesting to you than a piece of furniture!"

"No matter what I did or said, you never called me on it." He sounded furious. He could hear it. When inside he was nothing but cold. And he couldn't understand it. Or why he was still touching her like this, when he knew better. "I don't understand why. Why put up with it all this time? Why not tell me to go to hell?"

"Go to hell, Dare. Happy now?"

"You always used to fight me like you were three times your own size, Christina. Like you were larger than life. What changed?"

She sucked in a breath and he felt it as if she'd touched him. "You did."

"That's what you keep saying." His hands held her fast, but he noticed she didn't try to pull away. The heat of her skin seared through his palms, making it next to impossible to remember any reason in the world why he wouldn't do whatever it took to make sure he kept touching her. "But I didn't change that much. I got quiet, maybe. But you disappeared."

"I thought that was what you wanted." She didn't sound angry then, she sounded hurt, pure and simple. And here he'd thought he couldn't possibly hate himself more. "Something different. *Someone* different."

"The only thing I ever wanted was you," he whispered, as if it was a harsh condemnation of the both of them. "But I fucked that up, too."

And he couldn't handle the misery in her gaze then, slick and deep.

So he kissed her.

She tasted sweet and rich, the way she always had. She tasted like she was his, like she'd never been anything but his.

She tasted like home. The only one he'd ever known.

He kissed her again and again, and it was like the first time. Better. Promise and regret, apology and hope, and he didn't know what he wanted to get out of it. He only knew he couldn't seem to stop. He angled his head and took her deeper, tasting her and loving her and wishing this could be the beginning and the end of it. This kiss. This moment.

This.

He wished they could live right here, in this whirl of sensation, where everything made sense. His fingers sunk in the damp silk of her hair. Her hands pressed against his chest. That sweet little body of hers arched into his, fitting him perfectly, the way she always did.

He wished they could stay like this forever.

But that wasn't reality.

He pulled back, and saw an expression like agony move over her face, worse than that sheen of misery before. Harder to take.

"Why won't you tell me, Dare?" she whispered fiercely. "Why won't you tell me what's wrong?"

He didn't know what he'd say, there in that quiet foyer with a Christmas tree gleaming softly behind them, like the kind of blessing he refused to accept was real. He felt as if he was out on a terrifying precipice and the slightest little bit of wind could hurl him over the side, and the thing about that was, Dare didn't know which he wanted more: to keep up this balancing act or to let himself fall. He didn't know how to talk about this, or he would have. He didn't know what to say—only that he couldn't seem to do anything without hurting her worse.

"I'm not who you think I am," he told her instead. Gritty and dark. "I never have been."

"I think you're a pretty big jerk, actually."

He felt his mouth move, just slightly. "No, you don't. It would be a whole lot easier if you did."

Her face twisted. "Dare…"

But she never finished. Because the back door opened again, and Christina jumped back as if she'd been zapped with a cattle prod. Her parents' voices drifted in from the kitchen and he saw the yearning sort of look that was so foreign to him cross over her open features. He knew that Christina wanted nothing more than to run to her parents, tell them everything, let them help her through it. Through *him*. He'd never understood that kind of dependence on anyone. Even when his parents had still been alive, he'd spent most of his time hiding from them or perfecting the art of being invisible in plain sight. Christina's relationship with her family was yet one more thing about her that simultaneously intrigued him and baffled him. It made him feel like an alien creature set down on her planet from far, far away.

But today, he couldn't allow it. Whatever the hell it was.

"Not until after Christmas," he warned her, his voice low.

She frowned up at him, her mouth still soft from his. He could still taste her. He still wanted her, desperately. He was hard and angry and empty besides, and it was all her fault. And his, for allowing it. For perpetuating it.

"Since when do you care about Christmas? Much less protecting it?"

"I don't," he replied, that thing in him that felt like temper but he knew wasn't, not quite, sparking again and running deep. "But your mother sure does."

She mouthed something deeply unladylike with the same mouth that had just been lost in his, and he grinned despite himself as she stalked off down the hall toward the kitchen because *this* Christina didn't care if she pissed him off.

This Christina was the one he couldn't resist. At all.

This Christina was a Montana girl through and through, made of Rocky Mountain heights and long, cold winters, and she could take care of her own damned self. *This* Christina took after her mother, three parts ferocious and one part pure, humbling sweetness, and he couldn't seem to walk away from her.

No matter how hard he tried.

And not even if she walked away from him first.

CHRISTINA WAS IN hell.

There was no other explanation for it.

And kissing Dare certainly hadn't helped—if anything, it had made everything that much worse. She felt all the things she'd cycled through on the long drive to Marietta, from steely resolve to that hollow ache inside, but now she got to experience it all along with the crazy fire that was all Dare and that talented mouth of his roaring through her, too.

Making her feel as if she'd betrayed herself.

Making her want more.

Damn him.

She went out to greet her parents, playing the whole thing off as if this was a delightful Christmas surprise she and Dare had cooked up just for them.

"What a perfect Christmas gift!" her mother cried, wrapping her arms tight around Christina and making a whole lot of things feel instantly better. "And for your thirtieth birthday, too! I was so disappointed that we wouldn't get to celebrate with you!"

"We couldn't bear it," Christina said, which was true, at least. For her. And then she started in with the lying. "We had to come up."

"In two cars," her father murmured when it was his turn to hug her, and sling a welcoming arm around Dare's strong back. "One of which looks awfully over packed for a Christmas visit…"

But he subsided when Dare only smiled blandly at him in reply.

"Welcome home, sweetheart," her mother said, and Christina wiped the extra heat away from her eyes that *absolutely was not tears because she was a grown woman* when no one was looking.

Then the morning wore on, and life with it, even on December 23rd in her mother's tricked out North Pole of a house with Christmas carols blaring all the while. Her father went into the shop. Dare went to take a nap on the couch in the den after making his apologies for driving all night, as if he and Christina had planned it that way. And Christina and her mother baked the last of Gracie's usual Christmas cookies, packed them up into their tins the way Gracie did every year, and then took to the chilly roads to deliver the handmade gift baskets all around town.

Delivering Christmas cheer, Gracie had always called it.

This had always been one of Christina's favorite parts of Christmas, especially after she'd moved away from home, and today was no different. There was something about retracing the lines of this particular map of her childhood that she loved, deeply. It was like driving around inside her very own Christmas card. There were the actual streets of

Marietta and the roads that led up into the hills and off to the ranches, and there was the Grey family's own geography superimposed on top of it. And then Christina's personal memories of her eighteen years here like one of the filters she used on Instagram, bringing everything into a particular focus. The idyllic, the funny, the bittersweet, the faded into dim memory. All of it jumbled together into baked goods left on front porches or delivered to smiling friends and neighbors who more often than not had a gift for Gracie in return.

This never happened in Denver and after a few years of trying to replicate it in her busy neighborhood filled with young professionals who went elsewhere for their holidays, Christina had stopped trying.

Here on Bramble Street was her mom's best friend since they'd been kids together, who sent them on their way with her homemade hot chocolate in travel mugs. This pretty ranch had been in the MacCreadie family forever. This stretch of land belonged to nice summer people, the land over there to snooty rich folks who hid behind their dramatic gates and only emerged in fleets of Range Rovers, and that road led up to fancy Crawford House that was being made into some kind of museum.

It took her a long while to realize that she was homesick. And not for Marietta itself, though she loved this place dearly. But for those versions of herself she'd never get back—those ghosts of Christmases past who rode along with her in this SUV today, herself at eleven, fourteen, seventeen, so thrilled about what her future might hold. She looked out over the whole great valley and felt more lost, more adrift, than she had in years—since those first heady, unnerving weeks before she'd found her feet away at college on the other side of the Rockies, in fact.

"You seem so many miles away that you might as well be back in Colorado," Gracie observed as they headed back down from Crawford House. They'd left a present on the front steps for Mrs. Collier, the last grand dame of the once marvelously wealthy Crawford family, as she had always been the first to remind anyone in earshot.

Slumped there in the front passenger seat of her mother's Explorer, her hot chocolate long gone, Christina kept her eyes on the view before her and told herself it was the cold, cold Montana air that was making her eyes sting again. Despite the fact her mother's heater was working just fine, blasting too-hot air against her cheeks. There was snow up on all the mountaintops in all directions, but it was a shatteringly clear day today. That meant that this far up in the hills, she could see everything laid out before her as the winter sun catapulted itself toward the horizon. Her hometown sat like a perfect painting down there in the distance with the frozen river lazing its way through it, like a snow globe sitting pretty on a shelf somewhere, waiting for someone to shake it up.

"I'm thinking about geography," she said after a moment or two.

"Are you really?" Her mother laughed. "Not that there's anything wrong with geography, of course. I don't mean to laugh."

"I just mean... the maps that we make out of our lives. Mine started here."

She could see all the way across the valley to the far hills. The evergreens bristled but the rest of the trees were bare, and she knew this view so well. So very well. She could have drawn it with her eyes closed. She knew every craggy dip and turn of every mountain, from great Copper Mountain looming at her back out to the Crazies and beyond. They were etched into her bones, her flesh, no matter how dislocated she felt just then.

And so was Dare, in much the same way, and she didn't have the slightest idea how to go about changing that. If it was even possible.

"Why didn't you and Dad go somewhere else? Why did you stay put?"

She felt more than saw her mother's considering glance. "We like it here."

"But how do you know that if you never lived somewhere else? How do you know what the right thing is if you never try anything but the thing you already know entirely too well?"

Gracie took a moment to answer, and Christina heard her own voice as it hung there in the quiet—a little too rough. A little too revealing.

Maybe a little more than *a little.*

"I think most folks are born with restless hearts of one variety or another," her mother said, sounding as if she was choosing her words carefully. "And they keep on feeling that restlessness until they find the thing that cures it. Sometimes it's a place. Sometimes it's a person. A career, maybe. The chance to travel where they like. It's different for everyone." She slowed to go around a tight curve in the old mountain road, and Christina breathed out as the sheer exhilaration of it—the mountain, the stark view, *Montana*—flowed over her. She'd forgotten that, too. "And your father was that thing for me, right from the start way back in high school. So *where* we were didn't matter as much, after that, as long as we were together. I always got the impression that Dare was that thing for you."

She didn't ask the obvious next question, and that alone almost brought Christina to tears. And this time, there was no pretending they were anything but tears.

"I don't know," Christina said quietly. "Maybe the thing changes. Maybe it was never *one* thing at all. Maybe both of us were kidding ourselves."

Gracie kept driving, but she reached over and put her hand on Christina's leg the way she'd done when Christina was a kid, and it was as good as a long, tight hug from someone else. It felt like pure, concentrated love in a single gesture, and she had to close her eyes against it, it was so sharp. So good.

But Gracie's words burrowed deep.

"Your heart has always been your compass, honey," she said quietly as she drove them back toward town. "And a good one. Let it show you the way home."

Chapter Four

CHRISTINA LET HER internal compass, which she wasn't sure could lead her down a straight path with illuminated billboards lighting the way, no matter what her mother seemed to think, take her out that night.

They'd all had dinner at her parents' house without mentioning the word "divorce" even once. Her nephews had charged around screaming bloody murder and enjoying themselves immensely. The dogs had maintained a canine chorus throughout, interspersed with begging. Luce and her father had argued about some political issue as if their entire lives hinged on beating the other into submission. And Dare had practically flirted with her mother as if he'd downed a bottle of charm pills after his nap.

It was the perfect dinner, really. Happy, silly, loud. Like a scene out of a family-friendly holiday movie.

Too bad, Christina had thought as she'd nursed one of her father's favorite artisanal beers from the new local microbrewery and tried to keep her smile in place, *that it isn't entirely real. That most of us are putting on an act.*

When the political arguments had waned, the dishes had

been done by committee, and the grandparents had taken charge of the kids, the three of them remaining had sat there around the kitchen table reliving the morning's *pretend you're happily married* conversation.

Or that was what Christina had been doing, as she'd scowled at the Christmas-themed centerpiece involving merry snowmen and dancing candles and had attempted to pretend she hadn't been *that aware* of Dare sitting *right there beside her*—

"Let's go out," Luce had said abruptly into the strained silence, as little boy feet pounded up and down the upstairs hallway overhead. "It will be like a Marietta High School reunion in every bar in town." She'd checked her watch. "Except the microbrewery in the old train depot, Flint-Works, which just closed. So, you know. The other two."

"Is the high school reunion aspect supposed to be a draw or a warning?" Dare had asked as he'd lounged there looking beautiful and out of reach, as usual—with the faintest hint of the drawl he pulled out from time to time. It had made Christina feel melty and weak, the way it always did.

It had also made her mad, because she'd been sitting in her usual seat at the kitchen table with a straight line of sight down the hall to the front foyer, where she'd kissed Dare earlier that morning as if she hadn't packed up and left him the day before. What had *that* been about? Was she really *that* weak?

But she hadn't really wanted to answer that question.

"Let's go to the inevitable family reunion at Grey's," Christina had said instead of succumbing to all the *melting*. She'd wanted to ignore Dare but instead, had fixed a glare on him. "You can be our designated driver. Thanks for offering."

"Planning to dance on the tables?" he'd asked, sounding lazy and delicious and something else that had wound around inside of her and hadn't felt anything at all like a *compass*. It had felt a great deal more like an engraved invitation. "Your uncle won't like that."

Christina was well aware that Uncle Jason's "no shenanigans" rule was practically law around Marietta. Historically, he hadn't restricted that rule to only his saloon, either.

"Yeah, but we're family," Luce had said impatiently. "He won't throw us out. That's our name on the sign too."

"You say that like Uncle Jason hasn't thrown out family before," Christina had pointed out dryly. "You, for example. More than once, if memory serves. Pretty much every single one of our cousins, especially Jesse that Christmas his own father hooked up with his girlfriend. Uncle Billy himself about a thousand times, come to that. Not to mention Uncle Jason's *own* kids, who actually worked there. The man is merciless."

"Oh," Luce had replied airily. "He's totally mellowed."

And that was how they all ended up in a crowded Grey's Saloon on Christmas Eve's Eve, with what appeared to be half the town of Marietta.

Luce, unsurprisingly, melted off into a sea of locals who Christina knew enough to smile at, but not enough to walk right up and talk to without a little fortification first. Fully aware that Dare was right behind her, she made her way toward the bar, prepared to catch her surly, obviously completely *unmellowed* Uncle Jason's eye and try to convince him to make her about twenty margaritas, STAT.

"You don't have to look for our troubles at the bottom of a glass, Christina," Dare said, entirely too close to the back of her neck. She fought to restrain a little shiver as her reaction to that stampeded through her, all fire and need.

"Because you're standing right here?" she asked him, perhaps a touch too sharply. "Maybe I just want to be blurry. Is that okay with you?"

She was being flippant and she spun back to gauge his reaction—and froze. If it weren't for the hand he shot out to steady her, she would have slammed right into the nearest good old boy.

And then, suddenly, she didn't know where the worst— *or best,* something whispered—of the wild sensation was coming from. His hand, wrapped over the curve of her hip in an easy sort of hold that spoke of an intimacy she'd almost forgotten had ever existed between them. Or that look in those smoky eyes of his, serious and direct, cutting straight through her.

"I'll take care of you," he told her, and it sounded a great deal like a vow. Chiseled in stone. Direct and real. "Whatever happens."

She jerked herself out of his grip, aware that her cheeks were blaring with heat, and equally aware this had nothing to do with the fact she hadn't taken her bright red, too warm winter coat off when they'd come inside. Oh, no. It was all Dare.

"I've heard that promise before," she reminded him, and she didn't care that they were standing in public. That she knew probably eighty-five percent of the people here, or their families. That the country version of the Christmas carols coming out of the jukebox wouldn't muffle her entirely. "Sickness, health. And so on. You're not a good bet."

And Christina hated herself when his gaze went dark. Something like tortured. And his beautiful mouth set into a solid line that made her chest ache.

He reached over and ran his knuckles over one too-hot cheek, and there was no containing that shiver, then. There was nothing she could do but respond to him, and she didn't know which one of them was more miserable. She only knew it hurt. It all hurt. And that shiver still ran deep, arrowing straight into the core of her.

His mouth shifted into something too painful to be a smile. "That's what I've been trying to tell you," he said quietly. "For years."

Then he dropped his hand, and there was no reason in the world that Christina should feel so lost again. So bereft.

"I'm going to get hideously, embarrassingly drunk," she

announced, because it was better than marinating in that sense of loss. Because anything was better than that. And maybe there was a little too much challenge in the way she said it, but that, too, was better. "Margaritas will be tossed back with abandon. Shenanigans will be pulled despite the Jason Grey hard line on that. Reputations will lie in ruins at my feet."

"Or maybe you could try one drink," Dare suggested. "Two at the most."

Except really, it was more of an order, Christina thought as she eyed him, noting the faintly arrogant tilt to his head. The Dr. Know It All pose, as they'd called it when they'd still teased each other affectionately about such things. She hadn't seen it in a long while, and she didn't want to admit that it warmed her up even further to see it now. And when she raised her brows at him, he smiled. Just a little.

"You're the designated driver, not the designated Dad, thank you."

"I'll keep that in mind." Dare's voice was low and dark. His gaze was still much the same. And she didn't understand how she could be *this* angry with him and *this* sad and still want him so much it felt like a wildfire surged, dangerous and uncontainable, right beneath her skin. "I'm going to check out the pool table. And maybe while you're sacking reputations and doing a face dive into a tequila bottle you might remember that you're a noted lightweight, and if you drink more than about a margarita and a half, you'll fall asleep. Wherever you happen to be standing at the time."

That was possibly the most annoying thing he'd said all day, because it was true, as their entire history together had proved more than once. *Damn him.*

"I've developed a major tolerance while you've been off at the lab," she told him, which wasn't exactly true. But he didn't need to know that, so she embellished further. "I drink a case of wine a night. Two or three, for all you know."

"On the couch at home?" he asked mildly. "Where you then… fall asleep?"

Christina rolled her eyes, ignored the low sound he made that was far too much like the kind of laughter she didn't think he was capable of any longer, and headed for the bar again. She peeled off her incongruously cheerful winter coat as she went, determined to charm her constitutionally uncharmable uncle into letting her get sloppy and even a little bit crazy in his saloon. The way assorted historical Greys and the town's rowdier denizens had been doing since the Gold Rush era, when Marietta had been chock full of miners and the upstairs of the saloon had been the province of prostitutes and their clients—none of them exactly famous for their good behavior.

But the bartender standing closest to her when she snuck her way through the crowd was not her uncle—who would likely refuse to make margaritas at all on the principle that this was a saloon in rural Montana not the goddamned ritzy city, now that she thought about it, and she was fairly sure he'd actually said that to her before verbatim—but her cousin Rayanne, one of Jason's three daughters and only a couple of years older than Christina. Rayanne was remarkably pretty. She had been when they were kids and she was even more so now. Her golden blonde hair waved down to her shoulders and she had the kind of body that made a white tank top and old jeans look like a granted prayer. Rayanne had the biggest, widest smile in the state of Montana, and one of the best singing voices, and Christina still didn't understand why she wasn't a household name after all her years in Nashville.

Rayanne threw her hands up in delight, then rounded the bar to hug Christina tight.

"I didn't know you were coming!" she cried, and she pulled back to kiss Christina soundly on each cheek. Then Rayanne glanced down the length of the bar to where her father stood, his arms crossed over his solid chest and his usual scowl welded in place. Jason Grey and his lifelong bad mood were an institution here, and for some reason it made Christina smile to see it. She couldn't imagine the place without him. "Dad told me about sixty times that it was going to be a cold, lonely Christmas with no one to talk to but the wind. I should have realized he meant that was what he *hoped* would happen."

She moved back around to take her place behind the bar again, stowing Christina's coat and smiling away the overtly appreciative noises of some of the gathered gentlemen as she did—and who could blame them? Rayanne moved like she was dancing. She was lithe and lovely and had always been like this, always *that* pretty and fairly bursting with happiness besides. She was always on the near side of bubbly, always *this close* to bursting into song, and those were only a couple of the reasons she was everyone's favorite cousin.

"Tell me what you want," Rayanne said, and rolled her eyes when Christina reached for her wallet. "Don't insult me. Family discount always applies, silly."

"On all seventeen margaritas that I want right this minute?" Christina asked dryly. "And yes, they're all for me."

Rayanne eyed her for a moment, but didn't inquire. Maybe because it was the holidays, and no further explanation was required than that. It was perfectly possible to love the holiday season with every inch of one's soul and simultaneously want to take a little vacation in oblivion, after all. That was the peculiar magic of the season.

"Why don't we start with one and see what happens?"

"I'm trying to get drunk here, Rayanne. Very, very drunk."

"That's not hard, though, the way I remember it," Rayanne said with her easy grin. "Remember that New Year's Eve when you and Joey were thirteen and drank the leftover wine from your parents' dinner party?"

She laughed, which told Christina that Rayanne certainly remembered it. She did, too. Unfortunately. Christina and Joey, Rayanne's little sister, had heard this story almost every time they'd looked at an alcoholic beverage in the presence of a family member since. And it had happened more than half a lifetime ago. Literally.

"I'm so glad I have so much family," Christina said ruefully. "On the off chance I forget anything, ever, you'll all be hanging around to remind me."

"Only about the embarrassing stuff, Christina. No one cares if you were a good person, or a good student, or saved kittens every afternoon. Your family is here to mock you and humiliate you and remind you of all the things you'd like to forget, forever."

They both laughed at that, and Christina looked down the bar again. Uncle Jason was giving a familiar-looking cowboy the kind of glare that could easily escalate into someone getting tossed out the front door. Reese Kendrick, the man Jason had taken in as a kind of surrogate son way back when and who now operated as the saloon's manager, was setting up drinks with his usual stone-faced efficiency way down at the other end. There were a couple other bartenders Christina didn't know who seemed remarkably cheerful at the surliest bar in Montana, and two notable absences.

"Where are your sisters?" she asked Rayanne. "Have they fallen off the face of the planet? That's Luce's theory, you know. Has she run it by you yet? It involves the Northern Lights, a couple of grizzlies and a possible Sasquatch, and a lot of references to the early seasons of Supernatural."

"Luce is out of her mind."

"This is not news."

"Lorelai's still out in Los Angeles doing that Hollywood thing," Rayanne said, sliding the margarita she'd put together in front of Christina with dramatic flourish. "It would have been far more convenient for me if her dreams matched mine and we could do Nashville together, but that's Lorelai for you. Always doing exactly as she pleases. And Joey's still kicking ass and taking names in New York. I'm just happy she went with law school rather than the entertainment business. She can take care of the rest of us in our old age."

Christina grinned at the idea that sharp, focused, not-even-remotely maternal Joey might take care of anyone. Ever.

"I don't know," she said, and then something flipped over inside of her and pushed its way out whether she wanted it to or not, that grin of hers fading as it did. "The older I get, the more I think Grandma might be right after all. We're all cursed."

She could have pulled it off with a laugh, made a joke of it, maybe, but she didn't. And Rayanne had been leaning against the bar, easy and loose, but at that she straightened. Something uncharacteristically dark moved over her face.

But it was gone so quickly that Christina was almost convinced she'd imagined it.

"I refuse to give Grandma the satisfaction of being cursed," Rayanne said with a certain firmness that her troubled gaze didn't match at all. "We're all going live happily ever after, Christina, just to spite her. You heard it here first."

Rayanne went back to tending bar, leaving Christina no choice but to face her own not-so-happily ever after. She wove her way out of the crowd that was packed four deep around the bar itself. Once she was free of the crush, she could see Dare standing near the closest pool table, looking like the man she'd loved for so long now she couldn't imagine what her life had been like before she'd met him. She could hardly remember it. In her head, it was nothing but vague, dream-like impressions of her mostly happy teenage years and then Dare, sharp and in stark focus, as if he was the embodiment of clarity.

She took a pull from her drink and let the tequila do the thinking for her. And when she saw a group of folks she knew from high school, she pasted on a smile that was only a little bit forced and drove down a different memory lane altogether.

And for a little while, everything felt almost normal.

They'd been here before. They'd done this. The night before the night before Christmas, with all the rest of the town making merry all around them. Dare playing pool because he'd never been much of a socializer and Christina catching his eye every now and again as she went about the important business of catching up with her old classmates and friends.

Margaritas made it way too easy to pretend that they'd

simply... slipped back over the rougher spots in their marriage to a kinder, gentler place that felt entirely too easy. Too natural. And fit much too well.

Christina laughed, and soon enough she wasn't forcing any of it. She caught up with the lives of old friends and heard all the gossip about everyone she'd known growing up. She saw her sister doing much the same, if more drunkenly and with a bit more emotion than was wise this close to Uncle Jason's temper, and figured what the hell. If Luce wanted to pour out her troubles in a public place, who was Christina to second guess her? She'd never understood the need for that kind of thing more than she did tonight. She danced a little bit with some of her old girlfriends when a fun song came on, teased and was teased in return by people she'd last spent serious quality time with when they were all still teenagers and now only saw once a year at most, and it was *fun*.

It was more than fun. She was feeling as close to happy as she had in years, light and buoyant, and maybe that was why she forgot herself. That and the margaritas. On one trip to the bathroom, she didn't see Dare at the pool tables. She assumed he was at the bar getting himself the appropriate pint of Coke for the driving he'd be doing later. And so when she ran into him in the little corridor that led to the private office and the bathroom only employees and family used, it was a surprise.

Except it didn't feel like a surprise. It felt... good.

On the jukebox, Bon Jovi begged someone to come home for Christmas. And Christina smiled at Dare as if he was still the husband he'd been all the other years they'd been right here in Marietta, in Grey's Saloon, on this very same night. As if he was still *her* husband, the one she'd loved so much for so long. As if they'd never lost each other along the way. It was a big and loopy smile, and yes, it was a little tequila-tinged, but it came straight from her heart all the same.

But Dare wasn't tipsy in any way, she noted immediately, much less lost on some nearly-Christmas trip down memory lane. He only gazed back at her, that dark thing in his smoky gaze and his mouth a firm, forbidding line she probably shouldn't find sexy.

That was the thing about tequila. It made everything feel like sunshine. Even this. Even Dare.

"You could smile," she told him. "It won't kill you."

"It might."

He didn't crack a smile, so she couldn't quite tell if that was meant to be a joke. But she was shot through with enough sunshine to not care about that the way she might have earlier.

"You're the one who wanted to pretend we were happy together," she reminded him, and there was no particular accusation in her voice. It was simply a fact. "This was your idea. You could have been sitting at home in Denver all by yourself if you wanted. You probably shouldn't have come all the way up here and agreed to lie about your feelings if it's this hard for you to crack a single freaking smile."

"It's never just a smile, though. Is it?"

It occurred to her that she wasn't necessarily thinking clearly—or at all—when her back came up against the wall of the hallway with a little *thwack*. She hadn't realized they'd moved. Or that Dare had moved and she'd moved with him without noticing, and there he was, leaning over her and getting much too close.

And the situation got out of hand, just like that.

"Dare…"

But she was whispering, and she had no idea if she was warding him off or begging him to come closer. Or to come home to her, just like the song.

"First it's the smile," he said, his voice a husky thing in the momentary privacy of the back hall. "Then all the things that come with it. You make me imagine I can be that man you smile at, Christina. You make me think that if I play him long enough, I'll turn into him one day. But what happens if I don't?"

"I have no idea what you're talking about."

She also didn't care. The hallway was dimly lit, his mouth was so close to hers as he stood there in front of her that it was the only thing she could think about. Then he flattened his palms on the wall on each side of her head and the world disappeared into that gaze of his, smoky and intent.

"You know where I come from," he said, his voice like a dark throb along the surface of her skin, then deep beneath it. "You know what that makes me. Why do I have to keep reminding you?"

"You were a kid who deserved better and a man who overcame a deeply crappy start," she said, not following him. But it was hard to follow anything just then that wasn't his mouth. "You were also an awesome husband for a while, but then you went deep freeze on me. That's on you, Dare."

"You're drunk."

"I'm tipsy. *Slightly* tipsy. And what does that have to do with anything?"

He leaned closer and Christina trembled, thinking he would put his mouth to hers again. But he didn't. He angled himself so his mouth was right next to her ear, so that when he spoke his voice shivered over her and into her as if his hands were running along her skin.

She wanted that more than she could bear.

"That's too bad."

"Why?" She hardly recognized her own voice. Tight and needy and breathless besides. "I thought you told me not to get drunk."

"But if you were, I might tell you all the ways I want you, because you wouldn't remember. You wouldn't hold me to it in the light of day." His breath fanned over her skin and she *wanted*. She'd wanted him forever. She thought she always would. God save her from the things she *wanted*.

"You wouldn't know."

"I already know." She didn't mean to move, but then her hands were at his hips, touching him as if she'd never lost that right. As if he'd never shut her out. As if his body was as much hers as her own had always been. She'd forgotten how good that felt. How *right*. "But that doesn't matter if you won't do it, does it?"

"Christina." Her name was like fire. It streaked through her, searing her to the bone. "I try so hard to keep you safe, especially from me, and yet all I seem to do is hurt you."

She wasn't drunk, but she wasn't thinking particularly clearly, either. And maybe that was a good thing. She wrapped her arms around that lean waist of his, luxuriating in the feel of the hard muscles she loved so much even through the long sleeved shirt he wore. The exquisite perfection of his finely-hewn back. He sucked in a breath and she tipped her head back, her face still caged between his hands on the wall on either side and her arms caging him in turn, and their gazes tangled. Held.

"Then stop it," she suggested, and then she lifted herself up the remaining distance, high up on her toes in her favorite old boots, and kissed him.

She meant it to be a sweet sort of kiss. A longtime kiss, heat banked, just to remind them both of all their history—

But Dare had a different idea. The kiss stayed sweet for three seconds, then he simply held her face fast, angled his jaw, and took it up a notch to pure sex.

Insane sex, like gas on an open flame.

Everything ignited.

Fire streaked through her. Carnal. Longing. *Hot.*

It was as if they'd never touched. As if this was new. Sex and desire, passion and need, swirled between them, illuminating them both like a whole block of houses wreathed in Christmas lights. She felt *bright.* She felt *electric.*

Dare shifted, stepping between her legs and making Christina wish she wasn't wearing jeans. That she could press herself against him right here. That he could be inside her *right now.*

And still, he kissed her. Again and again, slow and hot and perfect, as if he could do it forever and would. Drugging. Mesmerizing. Wild. It was dirty and beautiful. It was yearning made real. It was everything the past year or so hadn't been.

It made her broken heart feel strong and whole and mad for him. It was better than it had ever been before, and she had no idea how that could be. Only that it was. And that she couldn't imagine ever wanting anything more than she wanted this man. In all these years, she never had.

She slid her hands up beneath his shirt, reveling in the feel of his smooth, hot, muscled skin beneath her palms. She didn't remember when she'd last touched him and she didn't know when she'd get to do it again, so she had to make this count. She soaked him in. All that gorgeous male heat. That delicious tension in his beautiful body that made the ache deep in her belly pulse, then spread.

He was her addiction. And she'd wanted him for so long now, and had walked away from him thinking she'd never see him again. Thinking she'd never touch him again. Thinking this would never, ever happen again.

And it was almost Christmas. And he'd come after her. And she couldn't seem to take this as anything but a gift.

She pulled back, and that hurt. Dare's gaze was unfocused and hungry, and it made a deep, dark thrill course through her.

"Come on," she said.

She took his arm and pulled him back down the hallway, further away from the noise of the bar and the music. She passed the private bathroom and the office, and the second hallway that went on toward the kitchen. Before she made it to the exit, she found the small utility room and pushed Dare inside.

Christina was perfectly aware that she couldn't have dragged Dare here if he hadn't wanted to go. Maybe that was why she was trembling when she followed him in, locked the door behind her, and then leaned back against it.

"Christina," he said, his voice a low, sexy growl. She felt it everywhere. "You want to be real clear about what you're doing."

"No," she corrected him, and her own voice was barely more than a rasp. "I really don't."

And then she threw herself straight into his arms.

Chapter Five

A BETTER MAN might have thought twice.

But Dare was not that man. Not even a little.

He caught her, hauling her up against him and taking her mouth with his again, unable to stop himself. Unable to get enough of her. Unable to think of a single reason why he'd denied himself this—her—for so long.

A better man wouldn't have pushed her away in the first place, he reasoned, so he stopped worrying about all those dark and lonely things and lost himself in Christina instead.

At last.

He poured the tangled things he felt into every slick slide of his mouth over hers, because he knew he'd never say any of it out loud. How he loved her. How he needed her. How he was barely a man at all without her, and nothing like a good one.

He maneuvered them to an old chair that sat in the corner of the small room, then pulled her down to straddle him as he sat. She wrapped her arms around his head and kissed him, again and again, until he thought he'd never see straight again.

God help him, but he was tired of seeing straight if it meant going without her.

And Dare couldn't hold himself back. His hands relearned her, streaking down the delectable line of her spine to hold her against the place he ached the most with his hands hard against the curve of her lush little bottom.

And then he groaned into her mouth when she moved against him.

She was so hot, so sexy, so perfect in every possible way, it hurt. And most of all, she was his.

Christina laughed, a low, delicious sound that made everything inside of him go taut. Then she shifted back and slid to her feet, standing between his widespread knees, her pretty brown eyes locking with his as she tugged down the zipper of her jeans.

He watched her as if she was a meal and he was very, very hungry. He was.

She was the sexiest thing he'd ever seen. She shimmied the jeans down over her hips, then shoved them down her thighs along with a bright scrap he knew were her panties, and then she let out a small laugh.

"I haven't done this in a long time," she said, breathlessly. "I forgot about my boots."

"I know exactly when you last did this," he reminded her, because she'd done it with him. Only and ever him. She laughed again, and then let out a higher-pitched sound when he grabbed her and pulled her back to him. He used his foot to shove the tangle of her jeans and panties down further, then thrust his legs through the opening between hers.

And when he stood up, holding her, she slid into place against him and they both sighed. He turned, propping her against the wall behind them, and held her there for a minute as she crossed her legs around his hips.

But Christina didn't want to wait. Her hands were busy between them, on his belt and then at the button of his jeans, and he bit out a curse when she reached inside and pulled him out.

"You're killing me," he told her.

But she didn't seem to mind that much. She laughed against his mouth, shifted against him, and then he was thrusting deep inside of her.

Finally.

For a moment they stared at each other, as if they'd both forgotten, somehow, the sheer perfection of this. The slick beauty. The *rightness* of it. Of *them*.

Then Dare began to move.

And it wasn't a seduction. It wasn't graceful or elegant or any of the things she deserved from him. But it was honest and it was frenetic and it was *them*.

It was *them* again. Finally.

Christina shook against him, sobbing out her pleasure into the crook of his neck, and when he followed her over into all that glory only she had ever showed him, he told himself he'd never let her go again.

That he'd die first.

Because living without her was the same damned thing.

CHRISTINA WOKE UP in the middle of her favorite dream.

Curled up in a warm bed with Dare wrapped around her, his chest hot against her back, letting herself drift as she reveled in the way they fit together so well. As if they'd been made for precisely that.

It took her a moment to realize that if her eyes and mouth felt *that* dry and her head ached the tiniest little bit, she wasn't dreaming at all. And then another moment—or maybe more like ten—to actually open up her eyes and assess the situation.

She recognized the set of shelves directly in her line of sight, with all her father's favorite dark mysteries stacked up with more enthusiasm than organizational prowess, and it all came back to her. Leaving Denver. Being back home in Marietta. Grey's Saloon. The utility room in Grey's Saloon, more importantly. Then the rest of last night, which had involved another unwise drink slid at her by her unsmiling uncle. She'd only had a few sips of it before she and Dare had to tend to a rowdier-by-the-minute Luce—before Uncle Jason took care of her himself, still without cracking a smile, no doubt.

They'd wrestled Luce into Dare's truck as she'd speculated about Hal's parentage with all of Main Street and the frigid night, then led her into Mom and Dad's house, snickering as if they were all teenagers again as they'd snuck up to the girls' old bedroom. Luce's boys were already there, sleeping piled up in their sleeping bags on the floor like a heap of puppies. Luce had stepped over them in the careful manner of one who had done so many times before, then done a header on the twin bed she'd slept in throughout their childhood and had been out, just like that.

And it had been the earliest hours of Christmas Eve by then and the house was cool and still. Outside the windows, the stars were distant and cold, and still felt like great songs welling up inside her every time she looked up at them. The way they were supposed to, Christina had thought as she drew a comforter up over her sister. The way they always did back home in Montana on a winter's night.

Christina and Dare had made their way back downstairs to the den, where her parents had set up the pullout couch for them. They'd still been laughing a little bit as they'd undressed and gotten ready for bed, with a kind of easy intimacy that had made it almost seem as if they'd shared a bed recently. As if everything between them was as it ought to have been. If Christina hadn't known better, she'd have believed it herself. And when things looked as if they might veer back toward their usual painful conversation and strained silence, Christina had made the command decision to head that mess off at the pass.

Which was why both of them were naked this morning, she realized, after another handful of moments passed.

Not just any morning, she remembered then, as she inhaled deeply and smelled cinnamon and bacon in the air, but Christmas Eve.

Dare stirred behind her, then sat up with a big, lazy stretch, and then there they were, suddenly. Staring at each other on a crisp, cold Montana morning, with that sharp winter light bleeding in through the windows. No margaritas or tequila sunshine. No dark night with all those winter stars shining down, making her feel dizzy. No blurriness and no excuses.

He looked shut down again, more by the second as they gazed at each other. There was something she couldn't identify in those smoky eyes of his, and that mouth of his— that clever and beautiful mouth she could still taste on hers, and all over her body—was a resolute line. Christina wanted to cry. Scream, maybe. Anything to keep them in that happy, bright sunshine sort of place they'd found in the saloon hallway last night. Or the quiet, reverent place they'd fallen asleep in, wrapped around each other in a sweet tangle of heat.

Anything to keep them from sliding back into all that bitterness she still didn't understand.

"We didn't use anything," she blurted out.

That was certainly not any kind of going to the sun road for them, she was aware as she heard those words fly out of her mouth, but there it was. Sitting out there between them. She could have detonated a bomb in the center of the brightly colored comforter that stretched across the pull out bed and it would have been less destructive.

Christina had no idea why she'd said that. No matter that it was true. It would also have been true several weeks from now, when she would know if it was actually an issue.

Dare blinked. That was not a good sign. "When?"

"Last night. You didn't use a condom. Either time."

He blinked again, but otherwise did not move. At all. That was a worse sign. "And that's an issue because...?"

Why had she mentioned this? But she had. So she pushed on.

"Because we haven't had sex in such a long time that I went off the pill," she told him bluntly. "I thought maybe it was manipulating my hormones and that was why I *thought* you were shutting me out when maybe you weren't." She smiled, faintly. "It turned out, you really were just shutting me out, with or without hormones."

He'd gone very, very still. Alarmingly still. No wonder she couldn't seem to stop talking. It was self-defense. It was warding off his inevitable reaction.

"Then I thought that it would be great to lose those five pounds I could never shift while I was on the pill, because surely you'd notice and then maybe that would spark your interest. Or something." He was worse than granite then. He looked carved from ice, and she felt it creep through her, too, freezing everything as it went until she felt like the frozen river that wound through the town. "But then I got a little overzealous and lost almost ten and, no. You still didn't notice."

"You're not going to get pregnant, Christina. You can't." Flat. Harsh.

And she wanted to sink back into the warmth of the bed, pile the covers over her head, and hide. Or start this morning over again, anyway.

But she wasn't the wife he'd ignored all this time, not anymore. She was the wife who'd left him. She was the woman who'd claimed him because she'd wanted him last night in that hallway. She was the one who'd crawled over him in this very bed because she missed him—and she hadn't missed this.

She was done putting up with his shit.

"You don't know whether I will or won't," she pointed out, her voice as cool as his was harsh. "You're a scientist. You're not God."

"You can't have a baby. *I* can't have a baby. You know that. And that's the end of the discussion."

He flipped back the covers and got out of the bed, because for him it really was the end of the discussion. The way it had been every single time he'd shut down the baby conversation for years now.

Years upon years.

The Christina who'd *contorted* had taken that, mostly. She'd told herself that he'd come around. If she was good enough, patient enough, caring enough, *something*. If she could figure out how to reach him. If she could make him feel safe, or trusting, or whatever it was he didn't feel. But she was done with that, too.

"Fine," she said, perhaps a little bit flippantly. "So if I do get pregnant, should I assume that means you don't want me to text you down in Denver to let you know? That seems a bit much, even for you, but if that's what you want, that's what I'll do."

He looked something like incredulous, except much darker and far more furious, and it took everything she had to keep her expression bland.

"What the hell are you talking about?"

"I've always wanted babies, Dare. Yet you've refused to talk about it for years and I let you, because I thought you'd get over whatever your problem is." She shrugged. Also flippantly, as if she was wearing something more than the comforter and too many memories. "But we're splitting up. I don't care what your problem is. And I can love a baby whether you're in my life or not."

He paused in the act of dressing, his jeans at his hips but still unfastened, and she thought it was deeply unfair that even when he was doing this stonewalling thing he did so much lately, she couldn't keep herself from noticing all those fine, masculine lines of that body of his.

All of which she'd reacquainted herself with last night.

Not that thinking about that was particularly helpful, just then.

"You can't have my baby without my permission," he told her, in a very low and very harsh way.

And despite the fact that she would normally agree with a sentiment like that, if not the tone in which it was delivered, because she thought men and women should make these decisions together and that all babies should be wanted by everyone involved, surely, today she only sniffed dismissively.

"Then maybe you should have been more careful."

"You knew you weren't on birth control and you didn't say a word. *Twice.*"

"You didn't ask."

His jaw worked as if he was biting something back, and she couldn't help the near-masochistic thrill that moved through her as she imagined what that might have been. What other, terrible depths they could sink to. If this whole thing didn't hurt so much, it would be fascinating.

"Is this what this was all about?" he asked, his voice as grim as that look on his cold, shuttered face. "You lured me up here so you could impregnate yourself against my will?"

"Oh, go to hell," she snapped at him then, and she realized she was shaking. That however masochistic the thrill of this on some level, the reality of it just left scars.

"I grew up in hell," he gritted out at her. "And now I carry it with me wherever I go. Why don't you get that? Why don't you understand?" His hand moved to his chest, as if he was showing her whatever lurked inside it. Warning her. "I would never inflict this on an innocent child. *Never.*"

He sounded furious. As if he was holding himself back from exploding with sheer force of will. As if he could shatter things with his voice alone.

But it dawned on Christina that actually, this was fear. All of this.

And that made the fury drain out of her, as suddenly as it had come. It made the shaking stop. Change into something else as she gazed up at him.

"You're not your father," she told him, her voice soft.

The effect on Dare was electric. He jolted back a step. He even paled. Then he scowled at her, and the fury was back again and darker than before.

"You have no idea what you're talking about."

"I do know. I know you."

"You don't know anything about me," he threw at her, and she thought that was panic, not temper. "Because if you did, you would have run a long time ago. You would have escaped."

"But I didn't."

"You didn't, and now look where we are. You packed up your car and left me without a word. We had sex in a goddamned supply closet in the back of a bar."

"It's the utility room in a saloon. Far less tacky."

"This isn't a joke, Christina."

She had never felt less like joking in her whole life.

"You," she said, holding his gaze, her own deadly serious,

"are not your father, Dare. Not in any way. You never have been and you never will be, no matter how you punish yourself. Or me."

She saw that wash over him. And then she saw him reject it. He straightened, his expression going darker and grimmer than she'd ever seen it, and he pulled on the rest of the clothes he'd left in a pile on the floor last night. He shrugged into his coat and grabbed his keys, and he didn't look at her when he walked out the door.

But he didn't slam it on his way out, either.

Christina sat there for a long while, not the least bit sure how she felt about anything. Not sure if she'd fallen apart already, or was about to, or was entirely too wrecked to fall any further.

Eventually, the prospect—and tantalizing scent—of a home cooked breakfast won out over all considerations, so she pulled herself out of the bed. Her parents had brought her duffel bag downstairs while she'd been out the night before, and so, when she stood there for a moment without shattering into a million pieces, she rummaged around until she found a pair of decent yoga pants and a sweatshirt. Plus her mother's awful bright blue wool socks, of course. She yanked off the sheets and the comforter, then reassembled the couch. She tied her hair in a serviceable knot at the back of her neck, made herself smile, and then went out to join her family.

Or the part of her family that wasn't Dare, anyway. Because she might not have heard his truck drive off but she knew that there was no way he was lounging at the kitchen table making small talk with her parents while Christmas carols played on the radio and everything was calm and bright. Or the Grey family version thereof.

Her nephews greeted her with shouts of glee that made her feel like she'd won a lottery or two when she walked into the warm, bright kitchen, then shot past her in their own wild stampede, complete with barking dogs at their heels.

"They want the television," Luce told her from her place at the table, where she was gripping a giant mug of coffee like it was a life-preserver, all her gorgeous hair wound into a messy braid that fell over one shoulder. Only Luce could look *glamorously hung over* without even trying. "Though I'm sure they're excited to see you, too. Deep down beneath the prospect of unrestricted cartoons."

"I felt the excitement, definitely," Christina assured her. "No matter how deep down."

"That was nice of Dare," her mother piped in from her own seat at the table with the local paper, the Bozeman Daily Chronicle, and the Livingston Enterprise spread out before her and her feet propped up on the empty chair beside her. "He said he had a few things to pick up, but was happy to take my last minute marketing list, too. Saves me that one last trip to the supermarket. It's always a madhouse on Christmas Eve."

"He's a sweetheart," Christina managed to say, and she

didn't flinch when Luce's gaze swung to hers with all those questions she couldn't answer.

And still, somehow, she didn't shatter. She had no idea how.

She skirted around her father at the stove, where he was frying up bacon and wielding the pair of tongs that were his favorite brunch weapon, to pour herself a mug of coffee as big as her sister's and with twice the creamer. And to give herself a moment to breathe through the unexpected swell of emotion that almost took her down to her knees—bright and sharp and full besides.

But still, not a shattering.

Because she'd thought Dare had left for good. She'd thought that had been the end of them, that awful little conversation on a pull out sofa bed on a cold morning after such a warm night. She hadn't known how she would explain it, what she would say. Much less how she would survive it.

And it told her all kinds of things she wasn't sure she wanted to know that the news he hadn't left her for good licked through her like the sweetest kind of relief. Vast. Enveloping. Something like life-altering, if she let herself think about it. She didn't.

"Big night last night?" her father asked, sounding amused as he glanced at her, then turned his attention back to the sizzling strips of bacon in the cast iron skillet before him that was older than Christina.

"Yes," Luce said from the table in her dry, husky-voiced way. "Because partying under the watchful eye of your angry older brother is always the *most* fun."

"Fun fact about your uncle Jason," their father replied cheerfully. "He's soft as a marshmallow underneath. Cuddly, really."

There was a small pause. The only sound was a chorale version of "God Rest Ye Merry Gentlemen" from the radio and beyond that, the zany, animated voices of whatever cartoon the boys were watching in the den.

Then everyone laughed.

Louder than necessary, and maybe a little sharper than usual with all the treacherous things waiting there beneath, but honest and gut-deep all the same.

The way they had more often than not, growing up. The way, Christina thought then, they always would. No matter what happened to each of them individually. That was the point.

And finally, it felt like Christmas Eve.

MARIETTA WAS LIKE a goddamned Christmas card, another tradition Dare hated.

It was like some ridiculous, picture perfect rendition of all the things he'd never had and never would, and Dare couldn't figure out for the life of him why it wasn't in his rearview mirror.

What was he still doing here? Why did he have his

mother in law's marketing list in his back pocket? What was the matter with him?

He didn't have an answer to that.

All this time and he still didn't have an answer to anything.

And Marietta was like a taunt all around him, daring him to figure it out before he lost this, too.

He'd picked up a change of clothes or two in one of the are-we-quaint-or-are-we-fancy boutiques in town. Then he'd headed to the supermarket, where the Christmas carols were on an endless loop and it took him almost twenty minutes to locate all the things Gracie wanted.

But the worst part were the families, he thought. Crying kids. Stressed out parents. Threats and breakdowns everywhere he looked. Santa Claus wielded like a battering ram— and he remembered this part. The only difference between his family and the rest of the world, Dare thought as he waited in a too-long line behind an exhausted-looking father and two caterwauling toddlers the man had clearly given up on trying to soothe, was that the Coopers didn't *pretend*. No one had used Santa Claus to modify Dare's behavior when he'd been little, they'd just smacked him until he'd shut up.

He told himself that it was honest. That it was *better*, really. That there was nothing the matter with him, it was the world that had lost its mind and Christina right along with it if she really wanted to participate in this massive *delusion*.

But that didn't explain why his chest ached the way it did on the short drive back to the Grey's house.

He told himself he'd drop off the groceries and then get the hell out of here. Because it might feel like he was dead anyway without her, but that was better than the alternative. He needed to let her go before he forgot himself all over again and woke up another ten years down the line, after he'd well and truly ruined Christina and made certain neither one of them had any way out of the mess he'd made of their lives.

Dare already knew how that ended. He'd seen the inevitable conclusion of this kind of madness once the Cooper family virus had run its course on a cold March afternoon when he was fifteen. He still couldn't block it out of his head, no matter how Christina smiled at him or how she claimed she knew him—or worse, how desperately he wanted to believe her.

He'd never be free of his past, his parents, his blood. He knew it. It was the lens through which he saw the world. It separated him—and that was what made him a great scientist, he liked to think. He could observe from a distance, research without emotion.

But the things that made him an excellent scientist made him a piss-poor husband. How many more ways did he need to prove that to himself? To Christina?

You should have let her go.

Dare parked his truck in the Greys' wide driveway and

wasn't surprised when the back door opened as he was slamming the driver's door shut. He braced himself, but it was his father-in-law who jogged out into the cold, his usual affable, welcoming smile on his face.

"Thought I'd give you a hand," Ryan said as he approached, sounding perfectly friendly. There was no reason that should put Dare on edge. It was his usual holiday phobia, he told himself, rearing its ugly head again. "We really are thrilled that it worked out for you and Christina to make it up this year."

Dare made a noncommittal noise he hoped sounded at least as friendly, and hefted up some grocery bags. Ryan did the same.

"I know you're not much for the holidays," Ryan continued in that same easy way of his. "I can't say I blame you. Between my mother and Gracie, I never had a chance to do much but surrender."

He smiled when Dare met his gaze, and Dare had a sudden flashback to when he was still just a kid, really, and Christina had brought him home to meet her family for the first time. Ryan had smiled at him exactly like this. Friendly, certainly, but with a certain measuring distance in his gaze that reminded Dare, now he knew the family better, of ex-Marine Uncle Jason.

"Anything I should know about?" Ryan asked then, as Dare had known he would. He indicated Christina's still-packed car with his chin, his smile still in place.

And Dare didn't have the slightest idea what to say. He shouldn't have come back here. He should have escaped while he could and left Christina to pick up the pieces any way she chose. *Christina and a baby, possibly*—but he definitely couldn't think about that.

But he certainly didn't want to stand here with this man, who was the closest thing Dare had ever had to a real father, and talk about the thousands of different ways he'd let Christina down. Especially not when Ryan had told him all those years ago, in the nicest way possible, that he'd tear Dare's limbs off if that ever happened.

"Not much you don't know, I think," Dare said eventually, his voice as even as he could make it.

"More than I should and less than I'd like to, I imagine," Ryan agreed, in much the same way.

He shifted, and Dare braced himself for the hit. But Ryan only reached over with his free hand and clapped Dare on the shoulder, the way he had that first day. The way he always did. And just like every other time, Dare... didn't get it. His own father had never touched anything or anyone like that. With that affectionate ease that felt to Dare like peering over the side of a great, howling abyss, it was so foreign to him.

Still.

And he was still tense, waiting for a blow. The fact it wasn't on its way came a little too close to choking him up.

"I think you're a lost soul, Dare," Ryan said then, very

quietly. "And your curse is that you've always been smarter than any man should be, so you know that about yourself. So I'm not surprised that you took one look at my daughter and held on tight. I'd think you were a fool if you hadn't done exactly that. I did the same thing with her mother."

They'd shifted position, and Ryan wasn't looking at him straight on or touching him any longer. His eyes were on that beat up old hatchback Christina had always insisted they keep with its University of Montana Grizzlies sticker in the back window. And that ache in Dare's chest worsened.

"Is this where you tell me I'm not good enough for your daughter, Ryan?" he asked, not doing anything to alter that harsh note in his voice. He should have known the blow would come—just not from Ryan's fists. Ryan was far more subtle than that. *But there was always a hit.* Dare knew that better than most. "You're a little late. But I know. Believe me, I know."

Chapter Six

RYAN TURNED TOWARD him then, frowning, and Dare understood he'd said far too much, standing out there in the driveway in all the December cold with too much Christmas in the air, like a scent. And far too loudly besides.

But it was as if everything inside of him was that damned ache, and it was cracking him wide open from within and knocking down all the barriers he usually kept inside him along with it.

He couldn't seem to do a single thing to stop it.

"I was going to say I'm sorry to see you look this lost again, after all this time," Ryan said after a long, considering moment, when there was nothing but the cold air between them. "I'd thought that life with Christina agreed with you. Made you happier."

Dare felt as if there was a hand at his throat, choking him, and maybe it would have been easier if there had been. He felt out of control. Crazed. Not separated from things the way he usually was. The way he preferred. But tangled up in too many *feelings* he couldn't begin to understand.

"It does," he gritted out. And then, because he really

must be lost, or at least insane, "that's the problem."

"Ah."

They stood there in silence for a moment, and that was just one more madness to put next to all the rest. It was another bright, cold winter day. The mountains scraped up into the chilly blue above with their great snowy peaks, all the plump little houses on this comfortable street had smoke coming from their chimneys to dance sinuously in the stark branches of the barren trees, and lights twinkled from the windows in anticipation of the winter nights that came too soon, here.

Yet his lunatic father-in-law stood there in nothing but his usual flannel shirt, looking as comfortable as if he was inside next to the old woodstove. And the overtly cheerful world filled with *normal people* around them should have felt like a slap. Like a kick in the head, because living Christmas cards like this one weren't for monsters like him. He knew that.

But today, Dare felt it all like grief. Dark and profound, not a slap at all, but a weight. He didn't understand that, either.

"Christina has a heart as big as the Montana sky," Ryan said after a long while, when only his breath against the cold had indicated he was something other than turned to stone where he stood. "But you know this. She will love you until the day she dies, whether you love her back or not. That's how she's made, and the father in me wants to punch you in the nose for not worshiping her like the goddess I firmly believe she is."

Dare let out a sound that wasn't quite a laugh. It hurt too much. "Who says I don't?"

Ryan smiled. "Fair enough. No nose punching necessary, then, which is a good thing. That's more my brother's department."

He faced Dare then, his hazel gaze direct. Not unkind, but unflinching all the same. Man to man. The way Dare imagined fathers might look at their grown sons, not that he'd know such things from experience.

Dare found himself standing a bit straighter all the same.

"A man isn't necessarily put on this earth to be happy," Ryan told him. "But that doesn't have much to do with whether or not he's a good man. It's a choice. You make it every day."

"Some people are predisposed to darkness," Dare managed to say past that pressure in his throat. "They infect everything they touch."

Ryan's gaze was so kind then it made Dare think of Christina's this morning. *You are not your father.* And he couldn't handle it any better now.

"No," Ryan said, his voice quiet but bigger, somehow, than the cold or the sky or the mountains all around them. "It's a choice. And no one, living or dead, can make it for you. But the trick is, you must live with the choice you make."

He headed inside after another moment, still looking supernaturally unaffected by the bitter temperature. And this was Dare's chance. This was it. He could leave the groceries at the door, turn his back on this house and everyone inside it, and go. All he needed to do was get in his truck and drive. He could put miles and mountains and whole states between him and these people who kept tearing him apart, bit by bit, with all this wretched, undeserved kindness he still couldn't quite process. Much less believe.

And he could leave this grief—this terrible darkness that burned in him like the inverse of all the happy candles in all the shining windows on this quietly happy little street—behind at last.

But instead, he pulled in a jagged breath and he followed his father-in-law inside.

Big Sky Christmases were the same every year and normally, Christina loved them.

Her extended family started gathering together as the day edged over into darkness. The elder Greys' spread was out near the ski resort in Big Sky, about an hour and a half from Marietta, on about ten woodsy acres that backed up into National Forest land with achingly lovely views back down over the Gallatin River and on to the Gallatin Range.

A Grey ancestor had laid claim to the land generations back. For decades there had only been a small log cabin on the property, which assorted Greys had used to access all the skiing and outdoor recreation in the area. But when Richard Grey had finally retired from running Grey's Saloon and handed it over to Jason, his eldest son, as tradition dictated, he and Elly had started building the house they'd always wanted. The original cabin remained because there was nothing Greys liked more than their own history, unless it was arguing about that history. The cabin was used as a guest house or family overflow location these days, and the Big House that stood higher on the hill with more of a commanding view was a sprawling thing, made of log and timber that managed to be airy and open yet cozy all at once.

Truly, it was a beautiful house. And at Christmas it was nothing short of perfect.

It sparkled with Christmas trees in all the soaring windows, with decorations carefully chosen by Grandma, who liked just the right amount of fuss—no more and no less. Every room was quietly resplendent in her favorite fashion, surrounded by the warmth of the log walls and the heat of the fireplaces. Dare had once remarked that the house felt more like an upscale ski lodge than a house, with the wings that rambled off from the great room in three directions, but that was precisely what Christina liked about it. It was deliciously comfortable, yet big enough that all the prickly members of her family could interact with each other and also, crucially, avoid each other when necessary without either action being obvious.

Uncle Jason usually left the bar in Reese Kendrick's capable hands on Christmas Eve and came rolling in around dark, like the surly dark cloud of gloom he was. Rayanne was like his own, personal sunlamp every year, a smiling shot of vitamin D so bright it almost made up for Jason's... *Jason-ness.* That and the fact her two sisters hadn't come home to Marietta in years, much like Aunt Annabel, their mother, who'd left when the three girls were teenagers and had never returned. Not that anyone dared mention her in Jason's hearing. At least, not while entirely sober.

Uncle Billy, the second Grey son, and his third wife, Angelique—who had first met the family while home for a different Christmas with Billy's son, Jesse—had come in the night before from Billings with their twin toddlers. Billy's other children, especially Jesse, tended to spend Christmas with their embittered mother on the other side of the Bitterroots in Idaho, where they no doubt discussed the fact that Angelique was just about the same age as Billy's own daughters. Another topic no one mentioned directly in Billy or Angelique's presence—because the only person who might get a pass on that topic, Jesse, had steadfastly refused to speak to either one of them since Angelique's defection.

Aunt Melody, the baby of Grandma and Grandpa's nuclear family, usually swept in sometime during the day in her hippie-dippy way that drove every other member of her family insane which was, she'd once suggested to Christina, why she enjoyed it so much. She was pretty in the way many of the Grey women were, willowy and blonde and effortless.

These days she was living in Jackson Hole, with a selection of men she liked to refer to as her *lovers* in front of her horrified parents and brothers. Her two daughters were a few years younger than Christina and usually turned up themselves at some or other point on Christmas Eve after flying into Bozeman, where the fact they were the product of different fathers—one of whom Melody hadn't bothered to marry, because, as she liked to tell everyone, he was an outlaw biker who wore no such chains—was usually brought up in conversation by Grandma within the first five minutes.

"As if," Devyn, the oldest of Melody's girls and the closest in age to Christina, had complained last year, if quietly, "Grandma wants to make sure I haven't transformed into the biker bitch within since she saw me at Thanksgiving."

It was already the sort of controlled chaos that Christina loved when they arrived in the late afternoon, and Luce's boys immediately ratcheted that up to crazy as they whooped and hollered and ran around. Luce's dogs and Grandpa's dogs howled their greetings at each other. Glorious smells wafted out of the kitchen, meats and pies and sweets galore. Carols played from the sound system, Christmas movies were on in the TV room, and there were plates of food to nibble at on almost every table the dogs couldn't reach.

And everyone hugged and shrugged out of their coats and schlepped their things to the various bedrooms that had been allocated for their use, while Grandpa prepared drinks and in the middle of the great open central room Rayanne told marvelous stories of her fancy Nashville life that were really more like mini-performances, and probably not very true. When she was finished dispensing her brand of sunshine, all the assembled cousins gravitated to one side of the room while their parents—and Angelique—clustered on the other.

Christina smiled and laughed. She caught up with her cousins. She played with the newest and littlest as they charged around on their wobbly toddler feet and tried to get their chubby little hands into Aunt Melody's famous crab dip. She chatted about absolutely nothing important with her grandparents and avoided her parents. She watched Dare do the same on the next couch over, his smoky gaze almost sweet as he did the family thing she knew would never come easy for him.

But this year, it all felt like ashes and empty gestures. That miraculous sense she'd had at breakfast that everything would be all right, somehow, was there still—but stretched thin. It was something to do with the stiff way Dare was holding himself. With the way he'd managed to avoid speaking to her alone all day, which was quite a feat, when she thought about it.

She tried not to think about it. And she tried not to drink too much of her grandfather's wicked egg nog, either, because she already knew how little *that* would solve. If anything, she hurt worse today than she had before she'd had the bright, tequila-infused idea to have sex with Dare last night.

Sex had never been their problem. It was everything else around the sex that had messed them up. Why hadn't she kept that in mind? Why hadn't she thought a little bit more about what today would feel like in the wake of more sex with Dare that *felt* life-altering but was, in fact, just... sex.

Christina understood that he acted the way he did because he was afraid. She even felt for him. But that revelation, like everything else, changed nothing, did it? They were still sitting here in the middle of all this light and laughter, alone. Apart. Maybe it was time to accept that this was how it would always be. That Dare had been right all along. That this could never, ever be anything else.

She drained her egg nog in a single gulp and told herself she felt *free,* not *depressed.*

Grandma announced that dinner would be in about thirty minutes, which meant everyone peeled off to their respective rooms for a little breather before the rest of the evening. Dare was nowhere to be found when Christina pushed her way into the cozy little room on the far side of the house, down on the ground floor with its own little deck looking out toward the mountains. She told herself it didn't matter. That she didn't care where he was. That they had only one more day to get through and then they'd be free of each other anyway.

Just like she told herself that the surging emotion inside of her then was *joy,* damn it, at the prospect.

She changed into a slightly dressier sweater, brushed her hair, and was considering applying make up for the sole purpose of making herself feel less frumpy next to all her naturally gorgeous blonde relatives when she heard the door open.

"Careful," she said from inside the bathroom when she saw Dare appear in the mirror. "We're all alone in here. You might actually have to talk to me. And then who knows what might happen? The world could end."

He came up behind her and stood much too close, pressing his chest into her back. And Christina knew she should push him away. She knew she should tell him exactly what she thought of his crap this morning, of his position on a possible pregnancy, and the fact she'd thought he'd bailed on her.

But she didn't say a word.

She only stood there, her eyes fixed on his in the mirror. On the two of them. He was so beautiful, still so damned beautiful, and when his arms came up to sneak around her, she felt beautiful too. She felt his heat and his strength, blasting deep beneath her skin. In the mirror, they looked like they fit each other perfectly. In the mirror, they looked connected and breathless and *alive.*

In the mirror, they looked like they were still in love.

And it was Christmas Eve. And she missed him. And she was losing him, more and more, with every breath they took, and she honestly didn't know how she was going to survive this. Him. The end of *them*.

"You don't have to pretend when we're alone," she whispered. Because she had to protect herself—something she always seemed to fail to do around this man. Again and again and again.

His lips grazed the side of her neck. His arms tightened around her.

"That's the trouble," he whispered back. "I stopped pretending. And it doesn't make it any better."

She shut her eyes against that, and then, after a deep breath, pulled away from him. He didn't fight it, but he also didn't go anywhere. He looked hot and a little bit dangerous as he lounged there against the bathroom counter and watched her much too intently, in a dark button down shirt she'd never seen before.

"I like your shirt," she heard herself say. Absurdly.

His mouth kicked up in one corner. "It's from a Marietta boutique. Just for you."

"It's like Christmas came early."

"I'm not sure Christmas Eve actually counts as early. Not really."

Did she actually laugh then? She couldn't believe that was possible, but his smoky gaze gleamed as he looked at her, telling her she must have. Christina stopped playing with her hair and let it fall down around her shoulders, the red streaks looking brighter under the bathroom lights. And even though she knew it was a defensive gesture he would read too much—or just enough—into, she crossed her arms over her chest when she pivoted and faced him.

"I forgot about Christmas," he said.

Of all the things he might have said, she hadn't expected that. "Really? Despite all the trees and decorations and stockings and family and, I don't know, the fact we're standing here in Big Sky pretending to be happy?"

His gaze managed to be lazy and amused and much too dark all at once, and her cheeks felt hot. Almost instantly, and then her stomach flipped a little, too.

"I mean, the gift giving part."

Christina didn't want flushed cheeks. She wanted her stomach to stay put. She wanted him, yes, like a mindless addict with no will of her own, apparently—but if she couldn't have him she wanted this to be over. Didn't she?

She cleared her throat and concentrated on her temper, not the emotion kicking at her just beneath it. "You 'forget' that every year."

The air between them seemed charged, then. Taut and fierce.

"Are you suggesting that I'm a liar? Just say it, Christina."

She'd wanted to say it every year, in fact, but hadn't because she'd wanted to preserve his feelings. That didn't apply tonight.

"I'm suggesting that Christmas is December 25th of every single year. It never changes. It never hides from you in

February or makes you look for it in October. Always December. Always the 25th." She lifted a shoulder and then dropped it. "I think it's interesting that a man of science, whose entire life is about tracking tiny little details, manages to miss that. Annually."

His voice was gruff. "I don't like Christmas."

"This I know. Guess how?"

"Because I keep telling you I don't like Christmas?"

"Because every single Christmas Eve you have a panic attack about how you didn't remember what day it was—despite the fact that you've usually had six Christmas parties with various friends and colleagues by then—and then you download all your family issues all over me, so I can feel bad about the fact I bought you a bunch of stuff and wrapped it and put it under the tree I decorated all by my goddamned self because you claimed you were studying. Again."

Her cheeks were more than a little flushed then, and her voice was too loud for the confines of the bathroom, and Dare's gaze had narrowed dangerously with every word.

"I'm a terrible person, clearly," he said in that low, edgy way of his. "And yet you think we should have babies together. Maybe I'm not the crazy one here."

She released her arms before she cut off her own circulation and turned to head back out into the bedroom before she could do something worse than say things she'd held back for a decade. Like reach out to him. Soothe him. Apologize.

"It's fine," she muttered. "I took care of Christmas."

"I don't know what that means."

"What do you think it means? It means that while you developed a sudden deep and abiding interest in watching animated movies with my nephews, Luce and I went into town and I did all the Christmas shopping." She shot a glance at him over her shoulder, and her whole body pulled tight to see he'd moved to the bathroom doorway and was leaning there, looking rangy and dangerous and entirely too edible. *Stop that,* she snapped at herself. "But you can go ahead and give me a divorce, Dare. And look at that. Best Christmas ever."

She didn't know what she expected. Maybe for Dare to turn a cartwheel of joy? Produce papers for her to sign on the spot?

But instead, he watched her for a long, long moment that bled into another, then hung there between them. Something like sweet.

"If you're pissed at me, you should probably just say so."

"I assumed that was clear."

When he looked at her like that, her temper ebbed away. It left her feeling weak and wobbly. Too needy. Too precarious.

"That's the trouble, Christina," he said quietly. "None of this is clear. I don't know how to be the man you want me to be. I don't think I'm capable of it."

"I know you are." She didn't recognize her own voice.

Fierce and sure. "But you have to try."

"How can you possibly know that?" he asked, and he didn't sound cold then. He sounded as lost as she felt. "I saw all these families in town today. And I felt *thankful* that I'd never have to put up with that again. The lie of it. The fighting and the stress and the *ruin* of all that pressure to *pretend*."

"Not all families are like your family."

"Is it better to be like yours?" he threw at her. He raked a hand through his hair, leaving it in spiky disarray. "Every year they all come back here and poke at each other and eat too much and drink too much. They throw salt in old wounds and lie about history everyone else remembers the other way. They fight a little bit, they pretend they're all closer than they are and they pretend they mean it when they hug each other, and then every year they vow they'll never do it again. But they do. It's like Stockholm Syndrome, with pie."

His voice had risen during the course of that outburst, and Christina thought her heart had come to a halt. She couldn't breathe. And she couldn't summon up even the faintest hint of that temper any longer.

She understood, then. Temper protected her. When that ebbed away, all she felt was hurt. For Dare. For what he'd suffered. For the way it was still wrecking him now, and her too.

"Of course it's not Stockholm Syndrome," she managed

to say.

"Then what would you call it?" he demanded, his face darker than the night outside. "There's no other reasonable explanation for anyone to participate in this kind of wholesale delusion!"

She opened up her hands as if she could hold the two of them between her palms and heal them both somehow. She wished she could. "Love."

He pulled in a ragged breath, staring back at her across the polished blonde wood floor and the cheery expanse of the sleigh bed with its patchwork quilts piled high. As if that hadn't been her voice, but the ringing of a bell, loud and insistent.

"What?"

"It's called love, Dare," she said, simply. Quietly. With everything she was, everything she felt, because she understood, then. How lost he really was. How she must have failed him, all these years, if he still didn't understand. And how tough he was to have suffered this, all this time, thinking it was something so twisted. So wrong. "This is what love looks like. It's complicated. Sometimes it drinks too much and steals its son's girlfriend. Sometimes it picks fights. Sometimes it's ugly and scared and shitty. But it's still love. It comes back home. It believes its own promises and it keeps them, too, in its own way. Because it's love. And it matters." She wanted to hold him but she knew, somehow, he wouldn't let her close. She knew. So she put it in her voice, tried to hold it her eyes. "And so do you."

"Love shouldn't hurt," he gritted out.

And she didn't know when she'd started crying. Big, slow tears that made tracks down her cheeks, overflowing from deep inside of her, where all she wanted was to love this man the way he deserved, and be loved by him in return in the same way. She wiped them aside and focused on him.

On this. On them.

"Everything that matters hurts from time to time," she told him. "Love shouldn't cause damage. It should heal it. But that's the thing, Dare. Healing hurts, too. It all hurts. *Life* hurts. In the end, that's how you know you're alive. Isn't it?"

But she wasn't surprised when he didn't answer.

As if he still didn't know.

Chapter Seven

M UCH LATER THAT night, Dare stood awake in the great room while the house slept all around him.

The Christmas lights still twinkled in the trees that stood in the windows, so he could see his own reflection. And then the shadow behind him that was first nothing more than a darkness on one of the far couches, but which gradually became a surly Jason, walking toward him.

The older man didn't say anything as he came to stand beside Dare. And for a while, they stared out into the woods together. The night wore on. Outside, it was so cold it seemed to shimmer off the glass of the window, and the snow flurries that had been coming down on and off all night took a little break in deference to the wind.

"There aren't any answers out there," Jason said, long after Dare had given up on him speaking at all. "I've looked."

"Maybe I'm looking for different answers."

Jason didn't laugh. Dare wasn't sure he'd ever laughed or even could. But still, he managed to give the impression of laughter with only a faint tilt of his head.

"I doubt that."

"Do you have the answers, too?" Dare asked.

"I've been a bartender for thirty years. I have nothing but answers."

The older man took a pull of the beer dangling from his fingers and it occurred to Dare, suddenly, that Jason wasn't simply bad-tempered. That he was broken. *Sad*, even, and all the way through.

He blinked, not sure what to do with that revelation.

"Okay," he said instead, when he was certain none of that would show in his voice. He doubted Jason would seek or appreciate any kind of sympathy. "Tell me why marriage is hard, bartender. From your thirty years of experience in giving advice."

Jason grunted, then glared out at the night. "Marriage is hard because it's a bait and switch."

"Because…what? Women are evil?"

"First of all, my niece is not evil. Let's be clear."

Jason, Dare realized then, wasn't merely sad. He was a little bit drunk. Another thing Dare didn't think he did. Ever. Then again, no one was awake but the two of them, this long after Grandma had called it a night and closed down the kitchen.

"Agreed," Dare muttered. Because Christina was a whole lot more complicated and dangerous than simply *evil*.

"And second, you go into it thinking it's about the fun stuff. Sex. Love." Jason shifted, but still glared out at the darkness. Or maybe his own reflection. Dare couldn't tell. "But it's not. It's about intimacy. And intimacy is the hardest thing there is. Most people suck at it."

"Maybe marriage is what sucks."

"Marriage is an abyss. Two separate people go into it together."

"And only one comes out?"

"That's if you're lucky, dumbass," Jason gritted at him, shifting that glare from the night to Dare's reflection. And it felt like a punch. "If you're *lucky*, you figure out how to make two separate people come together into one couple. But most people are too busy clinging to their own shit to ever make that happen. Believe me. I know."

Because of his own doomed marriage, Dare thought. Because his own wife had run out on him years ago and had left her daughters behind, too, as if she couldn't bear the sight of any of them any longer. He couldn't imagine that—but then, wasn't he standing here trying to gear himself up to do the same thing, more or less?

He met Jason's harsh glare in the window's reflection.

"Because you're a bartender, right?" he asked quietly. "That's how you know."

Jason didn't say anything for a long moment. Then his mouth moved into the closest thing to a smile Dare had ever seen on his hard face.

"Because I'm an object lesson, asshole," he said gruffly. "And if you're as smart as everyone says you are, I suggest you learn fast."

He gulped back the rest of his beer and then, without another glance, he walked away and left Dare where he stood.

Alone.

No matter how much he hated it. No matter how much he wished he could be different—be that man Christina still seemed to see when she looked at him.

While outside, where it was already technically Christmas morning no matter how far away it was from dawn, it began to snow again in earnest.

THIS TIME WHEN Christina woke, it was to find Dare stretched out beside her in the cozy little sleigh bed.

She shifted, making sure that she wasn't naked again—that the egg nog hadn't led her down the same dangerous road as the tequila had—and found that she was indeed wearing the pajamas she'd climbed into last night. When, if memory served, she'd crawled into the soft bed alone because Dare had been engaged in a card game with her entirely too smart—and correspondingly smartass—younger cousin Sydney, who spent her life doing top secret things in Washington, DC, or so she claimed.

Christina rolled onto her side, propping herself up on one elbow, and looked down at him. She had no memory of him crawling into bed beside her, but the fact he had meant she could take a moment to study him while he slept. Her beautiful, smart, broken husband. She wanted to trace those dark brows of his with her fingers. She wanted to burrow into the hot hollow where his neck met his shoulder. She wanted to kiss her way across the lean expanse of his chest and follow that dusting of dark hair all the way down. But any of those things would wake him and she didn't want that. Not just yet. She wanted to bask for a moment. Catch her breath.

She didn't understand how she could love him so much, even when it hurt.

But then, that was what she'd told him last night. This, right here, as painful as it was beautiful, was the point.

She had to look away from him before she forgot herself and when she did, she gazed out the windows across the room and couldn't help smiling at the world outside, drenched entirely in white.

It had snowed in the night. A whole lot, apparently. Great drifts piled up against the house and as far as the eye could see the world was pristine.

And it was Christmas. And it was perfect.

Even if it was supposed to be the last day of her marriage.

Christina climbed out of bed and dressed as quickly and as quietly as she could, freezing every time she thought she heard Dare shift beneath the quilts. Then she snuck out of the room and pulled on the boots and coat she'd left down here near the back entrance.

She still didn't want to wake Dare. Not yet. She wanted

to pretend just a little while longer.

It was what she'd done all last night, she thought as she snuck out into the breathtaking morning. The rush of the cold swept over her, through her. She pulled the hood of her red coat up over her head and wiggled her fingers deeper into her gloves before she stuck them deep into her pockets, and then she set off through the deep powder, her breath loud and hot against the inside of her scarf in the still morning.

She kept going until she hit the edge of the field her grandparents had cleared, up high on the hill that offered her sweeping views over the valley below. The Gallatin River was a shimmering band in the early morning light, the trees looked soft and perfect all covered in snow, and the evergreens looked fully dressed at last in their brand new winter wardrobe.

In the distance, chimneys breathed into the chilly air from the scattered houses, and clouds over the hills hinted at more snow to come. There'd be no getting out of Big Sky any time soon, she thought, and it made her stomach drop.

Because the truth was, she didn't have this in her. This game. This *pretending*. She loved Dare. That was the beginning and the end of everything, and she didn't know how to live in this in-between place. She didn't want to leave him, not really, and not only because they'd failed to use any protection. But she couldn't stay. Not when it was all so awful and he still didn't trust her at all. Could she?

She still didn't know.

The traditional Grey family Christmas Eve celebration went on long into the night. There'd been card games and board games. A long, loud dinner and an even longer dessert experience featuring enough pies and berry crumbles to feed the entire state of Montana. Definitely too much egg nog, as had become clear when Grandpa and Uncle Billy had started singing Johnny Cash songs from the piano, which always marked the tipping point in any Grey family gathering. Before Johnny Cash? A controlled, if occasionally boisterous affair. After Johnny Cash? Mayhem.

Christina had left the shouting—over proper song lyrics, of course, which no amount of Googling could solve to anyone's satisfaction—behind and had padded into the den, where Luce had been sitting by herself with *Love, Actually* playing on the big TV screen in front of her. Christina had plopped herself down next to her sister, made her share her cozy throw, and tried to lose herself in her favorite Christmas movie. Quite as if she wasn't sitting in the same house as her soon-to-be ex-husband who she suspected loved her *at least* as much as she loved him, little though he might know how to identify it. Much less act on it.

Watching Hugh Grant's British Prime Minister find love seemed like an excellent way to avoid thinking about any of that too closely.

"Don't do it," Luce had said during a quiet moment in the film, without looking over at Christina.

"Eat more crumble?" Christina had asked lightly. "I can't

help myself. I think Grandma's secret ingredient is heroin. That's how addictive it is."

Luce had turned to look at her, their heads almost touching on the back of the leather sofa.

"Hal never looked at me the way Dare looks at you," she'd said quietly. "Not even way back in high school when he thought getting in my pants was a religious experience." She'd smiled faintly. "No one's ever looked at me like that."

"Luce…" She hadn't known what to say. "The only person Hal ever really loved was himself. You know that."

"I don't think you want to divorce, Christina. Not really. Neither one of you."

Christina had looked away. Back to the TV screen, which blurred in front of her, making it impossible to see what the actor who had once played Darcy in *Pride & Prejudice* was doing. Good thing she knew it by heart, all the risks people madly in love were prepared to take. When had she lost that? Where had it gone?

"He pulled away from me," she said after a moment. "But the thing is, Luce, I let him. Or I didn't do anything to stop him. What do you have if no one fights to save it when it disappears? Isn't that a divorce already, without bothering to say the words?"

"A divorce is when there's nothing left to save," Luce murmured. "And that's me, Christina. It was me about five years ago, if I'm honest. But it's not you."

"I don't think it matters," she'd said softly. "I think our

marriage needs a miracle, and I can't seem to conjure one out of thin air."

Luce had slung an arm around Christina then, pulling her close, and they'd sat like that for a long time, tucked up under the throw blanket together the way they'd done when they were little girls.

"It's Christmas," Luce had said when the movie was over. She'd stood and stretched, and smiled slightly as she'd looked down at Christina. "It's like that song—miracles will happen while we dream. Believe in Santa and he will come. You know how this goes."

"What if they don't happen no matter what we dream?"

"This is your life, not a Christmas movie. You can fix the things you break." Luce had grinned. "Make them happen."

This morning, out in all the unspoiled winter snow, Christina still wasn't sure. She knew they'd both played a part in breaking their marriage apart, no matter what she'd told herself. She stood out there on the edge of the field, staring out at this land she loved so much it felt as if it was a part of her. She let that ache in her spread out and settle in, and she accepted that it would stay that way. That it wouldn't change. That Dare was the love of her life—but that didn't mean she got to keep him.

She shut her eyes and felt her tears freeze against her cheeks. And when she opened her eyes again and wiped at her cold, cold face, she couldn't say she was *happy,* exactly, but for the first time since she'd looked at Dare across that bar table in Denver and decided to leave him, she felt okay.

She'd get through this, in whatever form it took. She'd survive. With or without the baby they might have made. With or without him, no matter how much that tore at her. Because some broken things needed two people to fix them, not one. And she was standing out here alone.

She'd told him that love hurt. That life hurt. Christina had never believed that more than she did just then. And sometimes, the hurt was all you had.

I can live with that, too, she assured herself. *I will.*

But when she turned back around to start toward the house and face this strange, make-believe last Christmas with Dare, he was there. Just standing there a few feet away near one of the bare-branched trees, watching her as if he'd been doing exactly that for some time.

Waiting, something inside her whispered, but she ignored the little leap her heart gave at the notion.

"It's okay," she said, her voice sounding brash and harsh against the pristine winter morning, as if the snow itself took exception to her tone. "I'm not going to ask anything of you that you can't give."

Dare looked almost haunted then. She let her gaze move over him, taking in every detail of him and hoarding it as if this was the last time she'd ever see him.

Because what if it was?

She couldn't let herself think about that, so instead she traced his features. Those marvelous eyes. That mouth. The jaw he hadn't bothered to shave since he'd left Denver and the beard that was growing in there, making him look as surly as one of her uncles. And as rogueish as one of the heroes from her beloved romance novels. She sucked in a breath and tried to hold on to that sense of acceptance she'd felt only moments before.

"Maybe you should," he said, his voice a dark scrape against the snow. "It's the 'not asking anything of me' that got us here, don't you think?"

She didn't know why that seemed to snake through her like an earthquake, when it was such a simple question. When, she told herself, she didn't even know what it meant.

But that was a lie. She knew.

"This isn't anyone's fault," she said, and her voice was a fierce thing to hide the constriction in her throat.

"I figured out how to be married to you," he told her then. A gust of wind blew the powder against them, but he didn't flinch. Or stop. "It was like dating you, really. It was easy. I know how to love you. I know how to have sex with you. I'm good at it."

She frowned at him. "Were we having a research project or a relationship?"

"I don't know the difference, do I?" he demanded, and she'd never heard that tone in his voice before. Not angry. Not lost. But ferocious all the same, and her heart kicked at her, as if it recognized what it meant when she didn't. When she didn't dare. "Research *is* a relationship, as far as I'm concerned. And I thought I was doing pretty well. But you wanted kids. And the closer you got to thirty, the more you wanted them."

"Dare. You don't have to do this. We don't need a post-mortem. What's the point?"

He shoved his hands deep in the pockets of his winter coat, but didn't otherwise move. He didn't close the distance between them. He didn't walk away. And it seemed as if the complicated blue sheen of those eyes of his took over the whole of the world.

"The point is that I've always been a bad bet. And you've always been the one person in the whole world who didn't think so." He laughed, though it wasn't exactly a happy, mirthful sound. "And I've never been able to figure out why. No matter what I told you. No matter what I *showed* you. No matter if I was hot, cold, mean, sweet. You loved me anyway."

"That's what love *is,* Dare—"

"Until you stopped."

Christina thought her heart quit. Her mouth actually fell open. There was nothing but Dare, and what he'd said, and the intense quiet of the snow-covered world surrounding them.

"I *never* stopped loving you," she managed to say, though it was barely a thread of sound, swallowed up by the wind.

"How would I know?" he asked her, his gaze intent on hers. "We both fight dirty and quiet. We're both good at it."

She blinked, then shook her head as if she was trying to clear it, the past year and a half whirling around inside her head like too much tequila. She felt dizzy.

"I'm not blaming you for anything," he said gruffly. "That's not what I'm trying to do here. But you should know that I think every single minute that you think you're in love with me is a miracle, Christina. And every minute that you're not? I want to make sure you can get the hell away from me and find someone better. You deserve that. God, do you deserve that."

"Do you want me to find someone better, Dare?" she asked, and she didn't know where her equilibrium came from, suddenly. How she suddenly stood taller. How she was calmer, somehow, when nothing was solved. "Is that what you came out here to tell me on Christmas morning?"

"I would rather die than lose you," he gritted back at her. "Obviously, or I wouldn't be here. And yes. I'm aware that I was the one who pushed you away."

"I let you," Christina said softly, because it was true and it was long past time she said it to him. "I posted pictures of the meals I made you to Facebook and then I ate them alone, and some part of me liked that at least I could say I was trying. I had proof. But you shut me out." She was whispering. "You disappeared, right in front of me, and I let you."

He let out a breath, as if he'd been running hard.

"I'm never going to think you made the right call, Christina. I'm always going to think you could do better than me.

Than this… *mess.*" He shook his head. "I *know* you could."

"And that's why you think we can't have children. I get it," she pushed out, aware that her hands had curled into fists inside her gloves. Because she did get it—she just hated that he thought he was anything like the people he'd left behind. "Because you think the only truth that matters about you is what happened to you in the family you left when you were eighteen. Despite the fact *I know* you'd be an excellent father. And how do I know that? Because most of the time, you're an excellent man."

"I think the Cooper family is a wasting disease that creeps into the bones and ruins everything." His expression was so cold then it made the deep snow on Christmas morning seem warm in comparison. "Or kills."

"Except it's been over ten years and you still haven't hit me. You've never hurt me at all. Your version of fighting is a year of silence or the occasional loud word, or sex we both like. I left you and I'm still alive. I'm still right here. Completely unharmed."

She shook her head at him, exasperated and emotional at once. Yet deep inside, there was something warm and bright doing its best to make itself a flame. Because he was here. Because they were talking.

Because she believed in hope, especially today.

"You're the scientist, Dare. You know about exposure risks and incubation periods. I'm going to go out on a limb and suggest that maybe, just maybe, you developed a natural immunity."

He let out another long breath she could see as well as hear, and there was absolutely no reason at all she should feel it like light, dancing over her face and all through her body. Making her feel buoyant. Different, in that single breath, as if they'd both been waiting for him to let it go.

A little bit like happy, even, though she hardly dared complete the thought.

"I have a radical suggestion," Dare said then, when moments had passed, or maybe whole eras. "Maybe it's the Christmas spirit. I don't know. It's not like I would recognize it either way."

"You'd recognize it." She didn't look away from him. She couldn't. "It feels like love."

He smiled then, and it roared through her, because it was a real smile. And it had been so long. It was more than light, more than the holiday spirit as it swelled over her and through her and inside of her. It was more than a miracle.

Or maybe it was all of those things at once.

"Why don't we stay together?" Dare asked.

And everything disappeared. The Big House in the distance, bright and gleaming against the backdrop of pure white. The snow bending down the tree branches. The cold all around them.

There was only Dare. There was only this.

There was only the *trying*, or what else did they have?

"Why don't you find a job you like?" he continued.

"Why don't we live where you want, for a change? Why don't we go completely crazy and have a kid? Why don't we work it out and live happily ever after?" His gaze moved over her face and felt like a caress. "These are only suggestions."

"What happens the next time you get scared?" she asked, though she didn't want to. She wanted to throw herself at him the way she had in that saloon. She wanted to declare them healed and make it so. "Will I have to leave you to get your attention again? Is this what we do now?"

"Well," he said, and that smile turned crooked. "It looks like it worked."

She tried to frown at him, but her features weren't obeying her. Her heart was a kettle drum and there was something singing inside of her, deep and true.

"I promise you this," Dare said, in that way of his that felt like words carved into towering stones. Like vows pressed into her heart. "Every time you leave me, no matter why you leave me, I'll follow you. And then we'll find our way back together. I don't think it matters how we fall apart, Christina. What matters is that we keep coming back together. Forever."

"Forever," she whispered.

And she would never know which one of them moved. She only knew that one moment they stood apart, separated by a few feet of snowy ground and all those things that had seemed insurmountable scant seconds before—and then the next Dare was taking her into his arms and pressing his mouth to hers.

And this kiss was a vow. A promise. This kiss was forever.

It was coming home. At last.

"I love you," he said against her mouth, holding her against him. Then he said it again. And again.

"I love you, too," she told him, and then she smiled.

She reached up and took his beautiful face between her hands, so she could fall into those gorgeous eyes of his again and again and again.

"See?" she teased him. "This is Christmas. It's about love, Dare. Messy and complicated and exactly what we make of it."

"It's perfect," he said gruffly. "We can make it perfect."

And then they walked back up to the sprawling log house beneath that huge Montana sky while the Christmas snow began to fall again, like a blessing.

Like a miracle, after all.

Chapter Eight

CHRISTINA WASN'T PREGNANT, and the weirdest part of that was how much it bugged him.

"I didn't think you wanted a baby right now," she said, because something must have showed on his face when she told him.

"I didn't," he told her. "Right now."

And Christina smiled that little smile of hers that suggested she knew the darkest things in him by name, and loved them all. He was defenseless against it. Against her.

He hitched her hatchback up to the back of his truck and drove them both back down south to Denver, and he didn't stop off in Gillette on the way.

"Why don't we?" she asked as they neared it on the highway "We can put a few ghosts to rest."

"There aren't any ghosts in Gillette," Dare said. "There are only sad people living sad lives who probably don't remember me anyway." He took the hand she'd had resting on his thigh and carried it to his heart. "The ghosts are in me, Christina. I'm the only one who's haunted."

Her hand clasped his, hard, and he pressed it against his

lips, his eyes on the road and her warmth inside of him like a song.

"Ghosts are only frightening when you let them scare you," she told him. "Otherwise, they're nothing but memories."

Dare wanted new ones. He wanted the memories they made together to be stronger than the past. Brighter than the darkness.

They took it slowly, as the winter melted into a brand new spring. Christina never went back to that job she'd hated, and they were both a whole lot happier for it. She took a class on freelance writing at the university and went for it, with Dare's full support. They reverted back to a Ramen and rice existence, but when she got paid for her first article, the picture she posted to Facebook was of the two of them dancing in their tiny kitchen, and it was real. Not a fake meal no one ate.

What came afterward, of course, was far better and unpostable, but she didn't seem to mind.

Life was pretty good by the time Dare finally graduated from his PhD program, and he was more moved than he knew how to express when a whole slew of Greys showed up to cheer him on.

"You all didn't have to make the trip," he managed to get out to Ryan at the celebratory dinner they had later.

"You're family," Ryan said, in that affable, matter-of-fact way of his that made Dare feel like a kid again. Or the kid he'd never been. "We love you."

And if he got a little choked up at that, Dare would never admit it.

They left Denver in the middle of June, headed back up north to a post-doctoral fellowship position in the same research facility in Hamilton where Dare had worked before. And Montana suited them both, so much and so well that it took all of a couple of weeks for Denver to seem like a long, strange dream.

The summer was a cascade of soaring, hot days and nights that stayed bright until almost ten o'clock. The dizzy joy of a short, sweet summer in a place where winter reigned. They took full advantage of it.

They laughed. They talked. And when they fought, this time, they didn't let the silence draw out and become more powerful than it ought to be. They didn't let it become who they were. They found ways to get back to each other.

And when fall came again and the temperatures dropped, they were tucked up in a house they both loved in the beautiful Bitterroot Valley, nestled in the foothills of the Sapphires with the Bitterroots right there to greet them in all their glory every time they walked out their front door. Dare was enjoying his work at Rocky Mountain Labs and hopeful he'd be offered a full-time position when his post-doc was up, and Christina had found a job at the local paper to go along with the articles she'd started selling with happy regularity to national magazines.

And when her birthday rolled around, Dare knew exactly how to celebrate it.

She came home that evening to find that he'd turned the entire house—which they hadn't decorated at all because, Dare had argued while knowing he had this planned, they were going to Big Sky for Christmas anyway and what was the point—into his own, personal version of the North Pole.

He'd wrapped evergreen garlands everywhere they could be wrapped. There wasn't a single doorway without a sprig of mistletoe or two. There was a Christmas tree in the living room window, fully lighted, if without the kind of handmade ornaments he knew she loved. He'd bought those weird, lighted reindeer and set them up on their front porch, and he'd even gotten one of her mom's Christmas cookie recipes so the whole house smelled like home. Sweet, sugary home.

He started the Christmas carols when he saw her headlights in the driveway, and he was standing there at the door when she came inside, so he saw it. That look of pure wonder on her pretty face, as if Santa Claus really had appeared out of nowhere and just for her. As if this was magic.

And that was the thing, Dare realized. It *felt* like magic. Maybe Christmas was less about his own ghosts and more about the happiness he gave to others. To Christina. Maybe that was the point.

"I can't believe this," she whispered, standing in their

COME HOME FOR CHRISTMAS, COWBOY

living room with the lights from the tree dancing over her face and the bright red coat she still hadn't taken off. "Am I dreaming? Did I have a stroke?"

"Hold that thought," Dare suggested.

He went to meet her in the center of the room and dropped to his knees, and her eyes filled with tears. Instantly.

"Why are you crying?" He was laughing as he looked up at her. "You don't know what I'm going to say yet."

"You already proposed, Dare," she told him, her pretty eyes still too bright and that wonder in her voice, making it husky. "I said yes and everything. Did you forget?"

"I haven't forgotten a thing." He took her hands in his, and gazed up at her. His wife. His world. "Happy birthday, Christina."

"You got me a whole Christmas," she whispered. "I love it."

"Yes. And I want a baby," he told her, and watched the tears spill over and splash down her pretty face to hit that big smile of hers. "I want our baby. Our family. I want to love the way you do, all in and forever."

She pulled in a breath that sounded like a sigh and then she sank to her knees with him, wrapping her arms around his neck and pressing wild kisses to his face, his neck.

And they got a little bit lost in that, for a while.

But eventually, they were stretched out on the floor in varying degrees of undress, both breathing a little too heavily.

MEGAN CRANE

"If having a family is even half as much fun as making one," Christina murmured, grinning down at him from where she sprawled there across his chest, "I think we've got the whole thing figured out."

He smiled, brushing her hair back from her face, and understanding that this was home. She was. And he had no intention of forgetting that ever again.

"I want a family with you," he told her, like a vow. "I want the chaos. I want the complicated love and all that laughter. I want handmade Christmas tree ornaments and Johnny Cash duels over spiked egg nog. I want the Stockholm Syndrome."

She wrinkled up her nose at him, her eyes shining. "As long as it comes with pie, you mean."

"Of course. The pie is the whole point."

Christina laughed. "I love you. I love this birthday. I love this life."

She was light and love and she'd showed him a way out of the darkness. She did it every day. She was the cure. *His* cure.

So Dare told her so, softly and with great care and until she begged him to stop—or not—all over that sweet body of hers. All over again.

And when they threw themselves straight on toward their future family at the most wonderful time of the year, right there beneath their own, shining Christmas tree, Dare got it. They made their own miracles, and they always would.

Because the greatest miracle of all was that they loved each other.

And that was forever.

The End

You won't want to miss more by Megan Crane …

Please Me, Cowboy

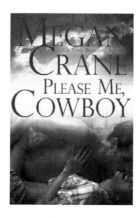

Gracelyn Baylee Packard got herself away from her dirt-poor Montana roots as soon as she could. Now – although she's never actually met the man – she works in Texas for billionaire Jonah Flint.

When Jonah summons her to inform her it's her lucky day, because she's going back with him to her home state as his guide, Gracelyn doesn't exactly see his proposition in the same light. So what if he needs her to infiltrate the tight community of a small Montana town to save his brother from a pre-nup-less marriage?

It's the last place on earth either one of them would ever go willingly, yet Gracelyn and Jonah discover that in Marietta they just might find exactly what neither one of them was looking for...

Available now at your favorite online retailer!

Game of Brides

Emmy Mathis is sure of three things:

1. Her sister Margery's three-week wedding extravaganza at their grandmother's Marietta, Montana home will be over-the-top ridiculous.

2. She'd much prefer to stay home in Atlanta in a pair of sweats.

3. And she absolutely, positively, won't feel even a hint of a spark for Griffin Hyatt, grandson of her beloved grandmother's best friend and the architect of the most embarrassing night of her life ten years ago.

But Emmy is dead wrong about number three. The moment

she and Griffin lock eyes again, the passion that's always smoldered between them flames. And they aren't kids any more, so why should they deny the desire that sears through them both?

Is this no more than a wedding fling between two people with too much chemistry and an overload of history, or can Emmy try to build a new life from the ashes of their past? And if Griffin is truly really free of his fiance, why is he a finalist in the town's Wedding Giveaway? Emmy can't answer those questions, but she does know that Griffin has the power to burn her like no one else.

Still, how can Emmy walk away from the one man she's always loved now that she knows what she's been missing?

Available now at your favorite online retailer!

About the Author

USA Today bestselling author **Megan Crane** writes women's fiction, chick lit, work-for-hire YA, and a lot of Harlequin Presents as Caitlin Crews. She also teaches creative writing classes both online at mediabistro.com and at UCLA Extension's prestigious Writers' Program, where she finally utilizes the MA and PhD in English Literature she received from the University of York in York, England. She currently lives in California, with her animator/comic-book artist husband and their menagerie of ridiculous animals.

For more info visit her at www.megancrane.com or www.caitlincrews.com.

Thank you for reading

Come Home for Christmas, Cowboy

If you enjoyed this book, you can find more from all our great authors at TulePublishing.com, or from your favorite online retailer.

Made in the USA
Middletown, DE
29 December 2020